The Julia Moriarty Trilogy
Copyright © 2014
Dick Gillman
Lanmeur
France

ISBN - 9781500943028

Cover images courtesy of Flickr

Front cover: Jun'ichiro Seyama – using 'Average Face' for iPhone
Rear cover: Painting by J. Cave, 1896 from page 29 of "Nearly three hundred valuable paintings of the American and foreign schools" (1917)

Sherlock Holmes

-

The Julia Moriarty

Trilogy

1894 - 1899

by Dick Gillman

iii

This is a collection of the first three stories that I wrote after introducing the character of Julia Moriarty. Holmes and Watson become acutely aware of her existence in 1894 in the story aptly recorded by Watson as that of 'The Shadow of James Moriarty'.

In the two stories that follow, Watson goes on to describe how their paths cross again. In 1897, he recalls the case of 'The Highgate Magician' and in 1899, he describes their further meeting in the case of 'The Severed Finger'.

Dick Gillman, 2014

The Shadow of James Moriarty

Table of Contents

The Shadow of James Moriarty

Chapter 1 - A Christmas Gift

An explosive event on Holmes's 41st birthday began the case I have recorded here as 'The Shadow of James Moriarty'. Since Moriarty's death there had been no-one to adequately challenge Holmes's formidable intellect...until now. It seemed like the very shadow of Moriarty himself was to envelop Holmes and take him from us.

It was a bright, sunny morning in the middle of December 1894 when I recall that I was in need of a Christmas present for Holmes. Sitting back in his chair, oblivious to the world, Holmes was conducting some piece of music with the stem of his pipe. "Holmes old man, I am at a loss as to what to buy you as a Christmas gift. Are you in need of anything in particular?"

Holmes stopped conducting and seemed to be giving my request some serious thought. Holmes held his forefinger aloft before replying, "Well, I did have a mind to treat myself to a new pipe. I do so enjoy smoking my Meerschaum, however, it does tend to get so damnably hot."

"Hah!" said I, "Consider it done!" and with that, I decided that very minute to leave our rooms in Baker Street and take a stroll down Regent Street to Carlin's, the tobacconists.

The weather was uncommonly mild for December and I had decided to forgo my muffler, being comfortable in only an overcoat and hat. Carlin's was a long established retailer offering a multitude of tobaccos and cigars. Indeed, it was well known that several titled gentlemen purchased their cigars at Carlin's. A stream of carriages throughout the day could be seen depositing their owners who would then take the opportunity to sit on a cask of tobacco and partake of a glass of sherry whilst they purchased their cigars. I had many times visited this particular shop and also had taken the time to explore their Oxford Street branch, discovering new and intriguing tobaccos. However, on this occasion I required a Christmas gift for Holmes, something rather special.

Standing on the pavement outside the shop, I paused briefly to look in the window and admire their display of pipes, including Churchwardens, Briars and Meerschaums. There were humidors for cigars and a fine range of accessories that every self-respecting pipe or cigar smoker was deemed to require. I was attracted to a particularly handsome briar pipe that had a Meerschaum interior. This pipe purported to have the porosity of the Meerschaum whilst retaining the heat absorbing qualities of a briar pipe. So enamoured was I with this pipe that I found myself speaking aloud, "Ah, ideal! The best of both worlds!"

It was as I took stock of the wares on display, that I noticed, in the reflection from the window, a man who seemed to be regarding me closely. Perhaps his attention had been drawn by my outcry but as I turned slightly, he hurriedly looked away and shielded his face by reading his newspaper. Thinking nothing of it, I entered the tobacconists. At once I was captivated by the intensity of the odour from the myriad of tobaccos on offer. To a smoker, it seemed as though one had been transported to Aladdin's cave!

On the glass-topped counter, which ran the length of one side of the shop, were small bowls of pipe tobacco. Within each bowl could be seen a label, written in fine copperplate, that gave the name and the price per ounce. Behind the counter were banks of tight-fitting wooden drawers, all neatly labelled. From these, the sales assistants took tobacco before weighing out the amount the customer required on a pair of ornate brass scales. Cigars were displayed in large humidors where they could be bought individually. If more were required, they could be bought as a box from one of the stacks on display. I was overwhelmed! Looking around, it took me a few moments to navigate to the section of the shop displaying pipes.

Before me was a vast array of pipes, including Meerschaum, Calabash and Briars. Some of the Briars were plain and burnished whilst others had been carved into intriguing designs. Seeing my interest, an assistant approached. "Good morning sir. How may I be of service?" enquired the young fellow.

"Good morning. I saw in your window display a fine Briar pipe with, seemingly, a Meerschaum lining?" I turned slightly, pointing in the general direction of the front of the shop.

The young man nodded saying, "Ah, yes, I know exactly the one you mean sir." Opening a drawer, he removed from it a pipe identical to the one I had seen. I took it from him and examined it closely. It was indeed a fine pipe and I felt assured that Holmes would appreciate the dual qualities of both Meerschaum and Briar. However, it was priced at three guineas but it took me but a moment to make my decision and I determined there and then to purchase it.

Leaving the shop with my purchase safe in my coat pocket, I patted it comfortingly and continued my stroll down Regent Street. As I happened to turn into Haymarket, I noticed that across the street The Haymarket Theatre had on display a large poster. This I saw was advertising the premiere of Mr Oscar Wilde's new comedy 'An Ideal Husband' on the 3rd of January. "Capital!" I cried aloud. Holmes's 41st birthday was on the 6th of January and as I had bought the rather expensive pipe, I thought perhaps supper at a restaurant and a theatre ticket would suffice as a perfect birthday gift.

Crossing the busy thoroughfare of Haymarket, I discovered the ticket office to be open. To my despair, I found that the tickets for the 6th of January were not, in fact, on sale but could only be reserved. Upon the wall of the theatre was a seating plan and on closer examination, I decided that a pair of seats at the centre of the Royal Circle would be ideal. A young lady could be seen in the ticket office; I approached saying, "Good morning. I would like to purchase two tickets in the Royal Circle for the performance on the 6th of January, towards the centre, if you please."

The ticket clerk reached down by her side and pulled out a large piece of printed card that showed the seating plan for the Royal Circle. The card bore the date of the 6th of January and from my observation, it was plain that many seats had already been sold. This was indicated by the purchaser's name being written across the seat. "I have these two seats together sir, in row 'C', numbers 17 and 18." The clerk pointed towards the two seats on the plan.

I looked at the plan and considered the seats' location in relation to the stage. In truth, they were a little to the left of centre but I determined that they would still provide a fine view. "Yes...yes, I will take those. Thank you."

The girl looked up saying, "What name is it sir?"

"Watson and Holmes," said I and watched as she wrote in our names on the plan.

Looking up the girl said, almost apologetically, "That will be ten shillings...they are the best seats though sir. You collect the tickets on the night from the box office." I nodded, took out my wallet and paid. As I walked away, I had the strangest feeling that the man I had observed in the tobacconist's window was hurrying up to the ticket office.

Chapter 2 - Silas Murchison

Christmas day passed peacefully at Baker Street. I presented Holmes with his gift and in return he gave me his. I watched eagerly as he unwrapped his pipe that he quickly filled and thoroughly enjoyed. For my part, I opened my gift and found a fine leather bound, silver hip flask which Holmes had generously filled with exquisite 18 year old whisky from his private barrel.

It was while Holmes was sitting back in his old leather armchair, 'breaking in' his new pipe, that I recounted how I felt I had been followed whilst shopping for his gift. Holmes sat forward in his chair, immediately concerned, "Tell me all you can of this fellow Watson."

I thought for a while, "Well, he was a man of average build, aged I would say around 40 years. He had dark hair mixed with grey and he sported long sideburns. He was dressed in a dark overcoat and had no hat. Other than that, I did not notice anything particular about him." I could see that Holmes was clearly frustrated by my poor observation of this fellow.

Holmes fumed in silence for a few moments and then threw his hands up into the air, crying out, "There must be something more you can tell me Watson!"

I turned to look at Holmes and as I did so, I saw a thread of burning tobacco fall from his new pipe and onto the back of his hand. Holmes cried out, brushing the hot shred of tobacco away. The tobacco had done no damage to his skin but in that instant I remembered something.

"Wait! Wait! I remember now. The man...he had a scar on his right wrist, a crescent-shaped scar, I saw it as his cuff fell away when he raised his newspaper!"

Holmes leapt from his armchair and began searching wildly amongst our files of known villains. "You are entirely sure of the shape of the scar and its being on the right wrist?" demanded Holmes as he continued to search.

"Yes, I am sure." I thought back to the event and I was confident about what I had seen although it had taken the accident with the shred of tobacco to bring it to the surface of my conscious memory.

After but a few minutes, a cry of triumph emerged from Holmes. "Ah, now we have him! Murchison! Silas Murchison. An extremely distasteful individual..." Holmes paused for a moment, his voice becoming cold. "and worryingly, a close associate of the late James Moriarty."

I slumped back in my chair. The mere sound of Moriarty's name brought back memories of evil that I thought I had buried in some deep, dark place.

"Moriarty! Surely not Holmes. There must be some mistake..." My voice trailed away, more in hope than in any real expectation of this being an error.

Holmes was now busily thumbing through our scrapbooks, clippings from newspapers that I had painstakingly collected and filed whenever there was a crime worthy of Holmes's attention. "Here's our man, Watson. There is a nice photograph of him after sentencing at the Old Bailey."

I walked across the room and held up the newspaper cutting towards the light from the window. The photograph in the newspaper was at least five years old and the paper had started to yellow but it was clear that the man whom I had seen was indeed Silas Murchison. "But...but why? What possible interest can he have in me?"

Holmes looked grim and I felt a cold hand begin to tighten in my chest. "I fear, Watson, that it is your association with me that has brought you to his attention. My concern is that Silas Murchison is not a man who is his own master. He requires direction. Someone is giving him orders and he has sought you out for some purpose..." Holmes raised his index finger and tapped it against his pursed lips. "Perhaps as a way to get to me...but who is driving him? You must be careful, old friend, I sense that there may be great danger close by. We must be on our guard."

I did as Holmes suggested. We were observant whenever we went out, ever mindful to see if we were being followed. I took to carrying my trusty service revolver in my coat pocket and Holmes took to carrying his heavy, silver topped cane.

We had had a fine Christmas. The New Year started with us toasting each other's health at midnight on the 31st of December to the sound of Big Ben striking twelve. We did little in the following days but on the day of Holmes's birthday, I believe he was a little surprised when no gift was presented. However, I saw a twinkle in his eye as he opened the birthday card I had given him as it contained a supper menu for the Hotel de l'Europe.

I could not resist revealing my plans: "I thought we might have a little supper in the West End this evening as I have arranged for us to go to the Haymarket Theatre to see Mr Oscar Wilde's new comedy, 'An Ideal Husband'."

Holmes's face was radiant. "But Watson, you are too generous. I have read a critique of the play in 'The Times' and any work that pokes fun at 'Society' and the hypocrisy of those in government is always welcome." Holmes settled into his armchair, still smiling whilst considering the supper menu.

Chapter 3 - Supper and a Show

By six o'clock we had dressed for the theatre and had descended to Baker Street to summon a cab to take us to the Hotel de l'Europe. It was just as I was sitting down in the Hansom that I noticed Holmes give the slightest of sideways glances. I was about to lean forwards to follow his gaze when his arm went across my body, preventing me from doing so. "What is it Holmes?" I asked.

Holmes's face was without emotion, "I believe we are to be followed and by none other than Silas Murchison himself."

"What? Where? Did you see him?" I blurted out.

Holmes face was now grim. "I saw a silhouette, and a figure which was plainly he, step out from a doorway and make a signal to a cab some distance away...but why this evening? We have not seen a whisker of this fellow since he followed you before Christmas. Why now?" Holmes sat back in the cab, deep in thought. I could see his fingers clasping and unclasping around the shaft of his cane and knew that the situation was indeed serious.

The cab clattered on through the streets of London and pulled up outside the Hotel de l'Europe, the supper house where we were to eat. As we alighted, another cab drove past us and Holmes gave the slightest of nods towards it. I watched as it drove on through the Haymarket.

Holmes patted my arm. "Come along, old friend, let us not allow this to spoil our supper," and he led the way into the hotel.

I have to say that for twelve shillings and sixpence each, the Hotel de l'Europe provided an excellent spread. Our first three courses included fillets of salmon, curried lobster; shoulder of veal garnished with forcemeat balls and roasted vegetables. For dessert I enjoyed a vol-au-vent of preserved greengages whilst Holmes seemingly had not had enough Christmas fayre and enjoyed a good helping of fig pudding.

Feeling replete and to aid our digestion, we walked the short distance to The Haymarket Theatre, a fine, white building designed by Nash and having a large colonnaded frontage. Soon we were standing in a small queue at the box office to collect our tickets. In front of us was a family, consisting of a mother and father, a boy and a girl of, I would imagine, 12 or 13 years and an elderly couple whom I took to be the children's grandparents. When it was their turn at the box office window there was something of a fracas. It would appear that the family had reserved seats whilst the grandparents could only buy seats some distance away. Holmes and I could not help but overhear the conversation and the poor girl at the window was trying to explain that there were no other seats available.

The father was pleading with the girl who plainly wanted to help but was unable to do so, "I'm sorry sir. You booked your four tickets in the Royal Circle two weeks ago and the only ones I can offer for sale today are in row 'D', numbers 5 and 6."

The father was almost beside himself, "But our tickets are for row 'C', my parents have travelled from Kent and we have come here as a family. Is there nothing you can do?"

The girl shook her head. Holmes turned to me asking, "Where are our seats Watson?"

I thought for a moment. "I believe they are in row 'C', numbers 17 and 18."

Holmes nodded saying, "Then let us see if we can be of some assistance." Holmes leaned forwards slightly and touched the brim of his hat, "Excuse me, may I ask what numbers are your seats? My friend and I have purchased seats in row 'C' also."

The father turned, clearly in despair, "We have numbers 19 to 22 but my parents are some considerable distance away from us."

Holmes beamed. "Fear not sir, my friend and I have numbers 17 and 18 and would gladly exchange them with those of your parents. I am sure their seats will provide us with an equally splendid view of the performance."

The look of joy that swept over the face of this fellow was something to behold. He grabbed Holmes's hand and pumped it as if he were drawing a gallon of water! "Oh, thank you sir, bless you, that is most kind." It was clear that he had been moved by Holmes's gesture, indeed, the whole family nodded and made plain their appreciation. Not only that, the girl in the box office was clearly relieved to have the problem resolved and smiled thankfully as she handed us our new tickets.

Chapter 4 - The First Act

We deposited our coats and hats in the foyer cloakroom and made our way up the sweeping staircase to the Royal Circle. After showing our tickets, we purchased a programme and quickly found our seats. In truth, from these new seats there was still a fine view of the stage and we quickly settled into them. I looked across to where the family was seated, some 30 feet or so away and as I looked, the children waved and I waved in return. The lights in the auditorium began to dim in preparation for the first act. I have to say that I found this to be something of a novelty. I had read in the programme that electric lighting had been installed in the theatre only a few years earlier.

It was some twenty minutes into the play, just as Holmes turned slightly towards me to say something, that there was a huge explosion to my left. It seemed to me as though an artillery shell had landed only yards from me. An object struck me hard on the side of the head and the force of the explosion caused me to be thrown bodily from my seat. I lay in the aisle stunned and partly deafened. It took me what seemed to be a minute or more to clear my senses and to take in the scene of devastation around me. I looked down my body to find that my white shirt was torn and completely covered in blood. Panicking, I checked my body for injuries only to find a woman's severed arm lying across my lap. It was the impact from this and the blast from the explosion that had felled me.

I shook my head in order to make sense of my surroundings; my hearing had not returned fully but I was beginning to hear faint screams. Looking around me wildly, I saw Holmes propped up at a strange angle against an uprooted seat. His face was totally white and there was a mass of blood around his right shoulder and chest. I must confess that I feared the worst. Somehow I managed to crawl, rather unsteadily, over to him. With some relief, I realised that his pallor was the result of plaster dust from the partially collapsed ceiling. I quickly examined him as best I could, my addled brain still reeling from the blast.

Holmes's eyes flicked open. I could see now that he had been skewered under the armpit by part of the iron seat frame that had been uprooted by the blast. He was clearly in great pain and I placed my hand on his chest preventing him from moving, saying, "Don't move, Holmes. I must see what damage has been caused." Some of the lights in the circle had survived the blast and had now been restored to full brightness. Opening Holmes's shirt showed a piece of ironwork, some three inches long, protruding from his chest. I feared that one or more of his ribs had been broken as the metal pierced him.

Grimacing, Holmes spoke, "You will have to pull me forwards Watson. It appears that the ironwork is still partly screwed to the floor." I looked at the iron seat frame and nodded. Fortunately for Holmes, it had passed beneath his arm as he was propelled sideways. It seemed that the frame had depressed the ribs, piercing only muscle and a fold of flesh. An inch or so to the left and it would have passed through his lung with fearsome consequences.

I took out my Christmas present from Holmes and passed it to him, "Take a couple of good pulls from that Holmes. I fear that removing you from this ironwork will be somewhat painful!" Holmes nodded and unscrewed the top of the flask. He took two or three good mouthfuls before handing the flask back to me. I took out my new, clean handkerchief that had been a present from my dear sister and splashed some of the whisky onto it. Wiping both the wound and the protruding ironwork, I braced my foot against an iron stanchion and looked at Holmes, "Ready?" Holmes nodded and gritted his teeth. I tried to pull as smoothly as I could but still Holmes yelped with pain. Once he was free, I clamped the whisky sodden handkerchief onto the wound. Leaning over Holmes's shoulder, I pulled up his shirt to examine the entry wound in his back. Thankfully, this seemed quite clean but as a precaution, I splashed a good measure of whisky upon it to cleanse it. In response, Holmes's body arched in pain as I did so.

I looked around me for the first time and was aghast at the destruction I saw. Where the family we had exchanged seats with had been sitting, there was nothing to be seen but a smoking hole through which I could see to the stalls below. Around me were strewn bodies and parts of bodies. Some of the injured were trying to move away, some like Holmes were trapped or had lost limbs. Staff from the theatre had now arrived and were trying as best they could to remove the victims to a place of safety. In turn, I struggled to sit Holmes in one of the relatively undamaged seats.

It was then that Holmes took my arm in an iron grip. "Look!" Despite his wound, Holmes raised his arm and pointed across the auditorium to one of the theatre's private boxes. There, illuminated by the glare of the electric lamps was a slim, female figure dressed in what seemed to be a black cape and gown. She was using a pair of opera glasses but not to look at the mayhem in the theatre or at the site of the explosion… she was looking directly at us! "Murderer!" yelled Holmes at the top of his voice, his arm still outstretched, pointing at the figure. People around us looked at Holmes and then looked towards where he was pointing. At this, the woman turned and fled from the box.

I looked around to see if I could be of assistance as there were clearly many injured needing medical attention but Holmes again grabbed my arm, "Watson, you must help me to get to that box."

I was shocked, "But, Holmes…what of the wounded? I am needed here!"

Holmes continued to hold my arm and he looked directly into my eyes. His voice wavered as he continued, "I must go there before the police trample all over the evidence…it is vital, Watson! Innocent people have died instead of me…because of me! I must, Watson, I must… or many other innocents may die!"

I could see that he was indeed desperate, filled with guilt and frustration at his own physical weakness. Reluctantly, I nodded. Helping Holmes to his feet, I put my arm around his waist and he placed his uninjured arm upon my shoulder. Together we stumbled through the carnage of the Royal Circle and began to follow the curve of the auditorium corridor that linked the circle to the private boxes. All the doors of the boxes had been thrown open. Holmes detached himself from me, and entered the second box and I followed. It became immediately apparent that this was indeed the box where we had seen the woman. I could see exactly the position where we had been sitting in the circle.

Holmes had fallen to his knees and I was greatly concerned, thinking it to be because of his wounds. I put my hand on Holmes's shoulder but he shrugged it off, "Fear not Watson. I have some strength left. I need to search for any possible fragment of evidence that might lead me to her."

I stood to one side as Holmes minutely and painfully scoured the floor of the box. Pausing in his search, he took from his jacket pocket an envelope and into it he placed a small fragment of paper from the floor of the box. Satisfied that nothing more could be gleaned from the floor, Holmes began to examine the four seats in the box. They were arranged as two pairs, one behind the other. Holmes ignored the rear seats and concentrated on the front pair.

"Hello…what have we here?" Holmes again took out an envelope and from the very tip of the arm of the theatre seat, he removed a few black threads. "It appears, Watson, that in her eagerness to leave, this person caught her gown on the domed head of an upholstery nail." Holmes rose painfully to his feet and I supported his forearm. "We must leave here quickly Watson before we are drawn into the investigations of Scotland Yard. I need the resources of Baker Street in order to make sense of what we have found."

I looked at the slowly spreading patch of blood that had seeped through the several layers of my handkerchief and onto Holmes's shirt. "Are you sure Holmes?" He nodded and mindful of my friend's wounds, we moved slowly. We made our way to a side exit, keeping away from the attention of both the medical assistance that was now present and the constables of the Metropolitan police. To avoid being questioned, we left our coats and hats for collection at a later date.

Chapter 5 - Examining the evidence

We were fortunate to find a cab at the edge of the crowd that had gathered outside the theatre and we were soon safely back in our rooms. Holmes was desperate to begin his analysis of the evidence he had gathered but for once I was able to prevail on a clearly weakened Holmes. Removing his jacket and shirt I saw for the first time the full extent of his wounds. From the bruising and swelling that had developed in the short time since the blast, it was clear to me that he had cracked, if not broken, several ribs.

I was relieved to see that the wound itself looked clean and I was indeed grateful that the Christmas gift that Holmes had given me had proved so useful for cleansing the wound in the theatre. Whilst only a flesh wound, it still required stitching. Holmes bore the pain well as I closed both the entrance and exit wounds. I had applied plenty of medical alcohol; my experiences in India and Afghanistan had left me in no doubt regarding the importance of thoroughly cleansing a wound. I had seen too many brave soldiers die from infected wounds. As soon as I had finished and had bound his ribs and applied a dressing, Holmes gently, but firmly, pushed me away. He was then to be seen reaching for his jacket containing the precious evidence.

Opening the first envelope, Holmes took a pair of tweezers and carefully withdrew the scrap of paper that he had gathered from the floor of the box. Using his magnifying glass, he minutely examined both sides before sitting back, deep in thought, holding his index finger to his lips. It is one of the mannerisms he has when his mind is engaged in considering a myriad of possibilities and utilising the vast store of information locked in his head.

It was perhaps two whole minutes before he spoke, "The box in the Royal Circle will, no doubt, have been thoroughly cleaned prior to the performance. Therefore, the evidence can only have come from the woman we saw. It is my belief that she is right handed, wealthy and has travelled recently by boat train from Flushing in the Netherlands to London, via the Isle of Sheppey…to be precise."

I was both amazed and stunned! The fragment of paper that Holmes had picked up seemed to be only a roughly torn triangle, barely one inch by half an inch at its widest. "But…how can you know this? That information cannot be printed upon what you found!" I spluttered.

Holmes smiled grimly, "The fragment of paper is part of a railway ticket. It is clear from the direction and the shape of the tear that the person was right handed. When one tears up a piece of paper, one invariably checks that it is no longer of value and one reads the contents first before destroying it. To read it, the ticket would have been face up. The tear can be seen to go diagonally from top left to bottom right meaning that it was held in the left hand and torn with the stronger right hand. The slight curve of the tear is formed as the right hand moves across the body." I nodded as I absorbed this information.

Holmes continued, his face becoming even more grim, "As it was discarded, this fragment must have fallen back into her open handbag. I believe that it was pulled out of her bag as she withdrew her opera glasses to confirm that we had perished. The ticket has a straight corner and then the rough edge of a tear. On it are shown the letters 'LC&D' and part of the following letter, which from its form, has a straight 'back'. Logically, the full sequence of letters would be 'LC&DR' which is the acronym of the London Chatham & Dover Railway. There is also part of the letter 'Q' shown as the beginning of the destination. Very few railway stations begin with the letter Q. However, the LC&DR have, as I recall, a station at Queensborough, on the Isle of Sheppey. This serves the boat train from the town of Flushing in the Netherlands. Finally, the colour of the ticket is a delicate shade of blue; this denotes that it is a first class ticket. Hence, she is a woman with ample funds."

I was once again amazed by Holmes's knowledge and powers of deduction. "Do you think this woman to be a foreigner?" I enquired.

Holmes thought for a moment, "I cannot tell. Perhaps the threads that I gathered may give us more information." Reaching for his jacket, Holmes removed the second envelope and painfully moved across the room to his microscope. It was necessary to light an oil lamp to act as a light source for the microscope and it was several minutes before Holmes sat back from the eyepiece, a quizzical look on his face. "Interesting, Watson. The fibres are fine quality silk from an expensive gown. On first examination, I thought them to be black but on looking closer, there is a mixture of both purple and black threads. You may recall, Watson, that this is the fashion colour for the new season both here in London but also in Paris."

I thought for a moment before asking, "So the clothes may have been bought in Paris or London?"

Holmes frowned, "I cannot be sure, but if coming from Paris, then the likely ferry crossing for London would be that from Calais to Dover, not from Flushing. This tends to favour London as their origin. Further enquiries must be made in the morning." Holmes sat and paused for a moment, "It is imperative that I send Mycroft a telegram regarding the recent release of English, or perhaps Irish, prisoners on the Continent."

"Prisoners?" I asked. Holmes nodded but would say no more. I did not press him further, I was acutely aware of his need to sleep and for his body to begin the healing process.

I awoke early the next morning and for once I was dressed before Holmes. This gave me the ideal opportunity to examine his wounds. I knocked softly on his door and found Holmes was dressed in his nightshirt and peering into the mirror by his washstand, preparing to shave. "Ah, Holmes, you are perfectly attired to allow your doctor to examine your wounds." Holmes grumbled somewhat but knew it was in his best interest to acquiesce. I undid the collar to his nightshirt and slipped it off his shoulder. The wounds, whilst red at the edges, looked clean and uninfected. The bruising, however, was continuing to develop on his thorax. There was now a fine array of angry blue and purple blotches but I was pleased with his progress and allowed Holmes to complete his toilet in peace.

Chapter 6 - Lady Elizabeth Crump

After breakfast Holmes began again in earnest. Taking up his pencil and pad he dashed off a telegram to Mycroft before ringing the bell for Mrs Hudson. As I filled my pipe, I remembered our final conversation of the previous evening regarding prisoners, "Tell me Holmes, why do you require this information from Mycroft?"

Holmes sat back and reached for his Christmas present, "It is because I suspect that the person who is trying to kill me is an associate of the late James Moriarty. In your opinion, Watson, why would this person wait almost four years before seeking revenge?" I scratched my head and pondered for a moment before Holmes continued, "Surely they would have had an opportunity before now…"

"Unless they were prevented from doing so…because they were in prison!" I shouted.

"Quite so, Watson. Even if they had been on the other side of the world, they would have been in a position to seek revenge in less than six months! No, there must be some particular reason for the delay. This person clearly has some villainous intent and I suggest that they may have been incarcerated in Europe, but why Europe…unless…" Holmes's voice drifted away as some new avenue of possibility seemed to open in his mind. "Quickly Watson, we have no time to lose. I must call on someone who may help us identify the sample of fibres."

Springing from his chair, as fast as his wounds would allow, Holmes grabbed an overcoat and muffler and made his way to the street below. Flagging down a passing Hansom, he gave the cabbie a very fashionable address in Kensington and in but a few minutes, the cab pulled up before a very grand mansion. Holmes paid the driver and swiftly made his way towards the front door. "Have a care Holmes. Be mindful of your stitches," I cried. I have to admit, this was more for my own sake rather than for any damage he might cause to himself!

Holmes had rung the bell rather energetically and stood impatiently in front of the large, blue painted, panelled door. He was just reaching for the bell a second time when the door opened. A manservant in full livery appeared looking plainly displeased. He regarded us in a very demeaning way from the top step saying, "Yes?"

Holmes had taken a card from his case and passed it to the servant saying, "Please be so good as to give my card to Lady Crump."

The servant examined the card and then looked down at us as though we were hawkers trying to sell furniture polish. "Wait here, I will see if her ladyship is available." With that, he closed the door in our faces. About a minute later, the same servant appeared with a much more ingratiating countenance. He bowed, saying, "If you would be so kind as to follow me sir, her ladyship will be pleased to see you in the drawing room." Holmes smiled and nodded and we followed him as instructed. The room that we entered was brightly lit and extravagantly furnished with gilt and velvet furniture. A large fire burned in an Italian marble fireplace centrally placed along one wall and the windows opposite had expansive views of the small park beyond. As we entered, a very elegant young lady rose to greet us.

"Mr Holmes, what a pleasant surprise." She held out her hand to Holmes who took it and bowed slightly, saying, "Your Ladyship."

Holmes turned towards me, "Lady Elizabeth, may I introduce my friend and colleague, Dr John Watson. Watson, this is Lady Elizabeth Crump."

I bowed, "Your Ladyship." Of course I knew of Lady Crump, she was a fine authoress and had penned many pieces that had been well received in literary circles.

Lady Crump smiled, "Dr Watson, I have heard so many good things about you from Mr. Holmes." I smiled a little self-consciously and mumbled a 'thank you.' Lady Crump beckoned us to sit before asking, "Tell me Mr. Holmes, what brings you to my home?"

Holmes moved forwards onto the edge of his seat, "Lady Elizabeth, I have a favour to ask. I would like to speak to your couturier in order to identify a sample of silk." Holmes went on to briefly describe to Lady Elizabeth the events of the previous evening and she was clearly shocked yet eager to be of assistance.

Lady Elizabeth rose and pulled on a silken bell rope and almost immediately one of her staff appeared. "I want my carriage to be at the front door in ten minutes, Pitt." The servant bowed and scurried away. Turning to Holmes, Lady Elizabeth said, "I am still in your debt, Mr Holmes. I will accompany you and give you a personal introduction." Holmes bowed and tried to explain that there was no need but Lady Elizabeth would not hear another word. Within minutes we were in her carriage and making our way to the salon of a famous Paris fashion designer.

As the carriage pulled up, Lady Elizabeth leant forwards saying, "Charles is an adorable Englishman who made his name in Paris but has opened the finest salon here in London." Holmes nodded and waited for her ladyship to make her way into the building. Once inside, the reception she received made it crystal clear that Lady Elizabeth was a frequent and well-respected client of this elegant and hugely expensive fashion house.

After a few pleasantries had been exchanged, Lady Elizabeth took the couturier to one side and discreetly explained the reason for her visit. I must confess that it was fascinating to observe his face. His expressions passed through a whole gamut of emotions: curiosity, surprise, incredulity, apology and finally, after her ladyship had raised her voice slightly, his face took on a rather submissive look. Samples of material were brought to Holmes who took out his glass and examined each one. "Ah, this is the one, Watson. Your Ladyship, I wish to know who ordered an evening gown in this material within the last month."

Lady Elizabeth asked the question and one of the minions was despatched to fetch the order book. The couturier opened the book discreetly at the page for December and angled it towards Holmes. He ran his exquisitely manicured finger down the page and pointed to three names. Lady Elizabeth looked over Holmes's shoulder and murmured, "I believe you said that the lady you are looking for is quite tall, slim and between 30 and 35 years of age?" Holmes nodded. Lady Elizabeth pondered for a moment, "Hmm, Lady Margaret….no, she is perhaps not of the stature you describe. Mrs Barbara…no, not quite the correct age. I know these two ladies but this third one…I have not made her acquaintance, Madame Julia Murphy, with an address of The Savoy Hotel."

"Murphy, you say!" I could see Holmes's eyes light up, "Thank you, Lady Elizabeth. You have been supremely helpful." Bowing slightly, Holmes turned and rushed from the salon, leaving me to follow in his wake, after muttering a hurried 'goodbye' to a rather bemused Lady Elizabeth.

Chapter 7 - A name to conjure with

By the time I had caught up with Holmes, he had already hailed a cab and we returned to Baker Street almost at a gallop! Holmes was clearly impatient to see whether brother Mycroft had acquired the intelligence he needed from the Continent. As we entered our rooms, Mrs Hudson appeared with an envelope in her hands. "This arrived for you a few minutes ago Mr Holmes, by Government messenger."

Holmes eagerly took the envelope and breaking the wax seal, he devoured the contents avidly. His cry of triumph quite startled me, "Ha! It is as I suspected!" Holmes was pointing to a list of some ten names; beside each one were the name of the prison and the date of release, together with the reason for imprisonment. "Listen to this, Watson: Antwerp prison, 1st December 1894. Murphy, Julia. Reason for imprisonment...assault with a knife." Holmes's eyes burned as he said "Madame Murphy sounds to be a particularly interesting and resourceful lady."

I sat down and began to fill my pipe. Again I was puzzled. "I have to say Holmes that I am somewhat confused. Do you now believe that this Madame Murphy is the person directing Silas Murchison?"

Holmes reached for his old Persian slipper tobacco pouch and began to thoughtfully fill his pipe. He did not reply directly, saying only, "There is a twist here, Watson. What do you know of the origins of surnames?"

I had to admit that I knew very little. "Well, I know that my own surname is derived from 'Son of Walter' but I am afraid that is the limit of my knowledge."

Holmes lit his pipe, sat back and then blew out a long, steady blue stream of smoke. "What would you say, Watson, if I told you that the surname Murphy meant 'sea warrior'?"

I thought for a moment before saying, "I would say that it is singularly unimportant to the case in hand."

At that, Holmes roared with laughter. "Watson old friend, I can always rely on you to lighten the darkest of situations. What then would you say if I were to tell you that Murphy is a derivative of the name Moriarty?"

I jolted upright as though I had been pinched. "What? You mean that Julia Murphy is in fact Julia Moriarty? She is Moriarty's wife?"

The smile faded from Holmes's face; it was now grim and he shook his head. "I do not believe so. As an academic, I do not recall any mention of his having a wife. I suspect that this lady is, in fact, his sister. This is pure conjecture, but I imagine that she has always been the accomplice of James

Moriarty, equal in intelligence and equally malevolent. She has stayed hidden in the shadows, her existence known only to the top echelon of Moriarty's sphere of influence. Only on her release from prison has she been able to reach out as James Moriarty's cold hand to try and destroy me."

I sat aghast. "Julia Moriarty…so she is the one who is directing the actions of Silas Murchison!"

Holmes nodded, "Yes, I suspect that she travelled with her brother to Switzerland. After my 'meeting' with her brother at the Reichenbach Falls, she fled, fearing that I might somehow have survived and had started a hue and cry for all her brother's accomplices. Somehow, she must have fallen foul of the authorities in Holland and lashed out, causing her to be imprisoned. Upon her release in Antwerp, she took the nearest ferry, that being from Flushing to London. Once here, she revived part of her brother's network of criminals and set about finding a way to take revenge for her brother's death."

Bearing in mind the events of the last few days, I tried to marry my own thoughts to those of Holmes. "So, when I went out to buy your Christmas present, Murchison was gathering intelligence for Julia Moriarty…and…when I left the theatre booking office, I was correct in my suspicion that he had followed very closely on my heels!"

34

Holmes drew on his pipe. "Yes, it was imperative that he follow quickly so that he could see which seats you had bought and for which date. That information must have been invaluable to Julia Moriarty. She now knew exactly where I would be, at a specific time and on a specific date. What better than to prepare a bomb to be placed under my theatre seat and timed to explode during the performance?"

I nodded, saying, "And that is why we never saw him again until the evening of the performance. There was no need for him to follow us further!"

"Precisely Watson. All he needed to do was to watch for us on the night of the performance. He saw us leave our rooms dressed for the theatre. He followed and then drove on to The Haymarket Theatre with the bomb."

I thought back to that night; how we had alighted from the cab at the supper house and seen the cab that had been following us drive past down Haymarket towards the theatre. "He must have reserved a seat in the row directly behind ours and then simply slipped the bomb beneath our seats!"

Holmes nodded. "Yes. Once in his seat, he would have started the clockwork mechanism of the timer and then quietly left the theatre. Holmes slapped the arm of his chair with the palm of his hand, saying, "It is the callousness that I cannot quite accept. She is quite prepared to kill innocent men, women and children to satisfy her need for revenge against one man. There is no honour in this!"

I stood and scratched my head in puzzlement. "But how are we to catch her?" I asked.

Chapter 8 - Preparing the bait

Holmes rose from his chair and began to pace slowly. I had the impression that a plan was forming in his head. "We have the perfect bait to lure her from her lair, Watson."

It took me but a moment to realise what he was saying. "You can't mean…No Holmes, you are still injured. You cannot risk your life!"

Holmes turned angrily towards me, his eyes ablaze. "I must, can't you see? If I do not, then she may try and attack me again in another public place and more innocent lives may be lost."

I could see the cold logic in what he said but to offer himself as a living target was difficult for me to accept. I was quiet for several minutes before finally accepting the inevitable, saying, "How is it to be done, Holmes?"

Holmes stopped pacing. "I believe that on this occasion, we have the advantage, Watson. We know where the lady is staying and we know that she directs the movements of Murchison. What if I were to send her a hand-written note offering to meet her alone and unarmed in order to avoid any further loss of innocent life?"

Without hesitation, I said, "She would flee when she realised that you had discovered her hiding place."

Holmes once more began pacing as he ran through the various scenarios in his head. "I think that is highly unlikely, Watson. I think she will readily agree. She will see it as my Achilles heel, a weakness on my part: the great Sherlock Holmes putting honour and innocent lives before his own."

I thought for a moment. "But is this not so? You are delivering yourself to this…this monster!"

A wicked smile spread across Holmes's face. "You forget, Watson. This time the game is on our ground, at a place and a time of our choosing. She will not argue. She is driven by revenge and for all her intellect, she is blinkered by that one thought…my destruction! This is our advantage."

The following morning, I found that Holmes had breakfasted early and had left our rooms. I took the opportunity to catch up on some reading and it was at around 10 o'clock that I heard our doorbell ring in the hall below. A few moments later, Mrs Hudson came in with a dirty, wretched fellow. With all the good grace she could muster, Mrs Hudson announced the visitor, "This is Mr Pargeter, Dr Watson. He claims he knows Mr Holmes."

I looked at the fellow. He was dressed in the clothes of a railway worker and was covered in soot and grime. His boots were heavily scuffed and upon his head, he wore a greasy peaked cap, beneath which a mop of equally greasy black hair protruded. He sniffed, wiped his nose on his hand before offering to shake hands, saying, "Howdya do?"

I took a step back, feeling safer to just nod a greeting. The man looked around our rooms. His face was caked in filth and was screwed up into an inane grin, his eyes almost slits. "Will he be long then…Mr Holmes? I only ask 'cos I has to be back at the engine shed by 11 o'clock."

The man made to sit down on our sofa and I had to rush to spread out a copy of 'The Times' on the velvet cover before his dirty trousers left an indelible mark. "I…I really don't know. He left early this morning and I'm not quite sure when he will return. Perhaps you might come back later, after work, when you have had time to bathe?"

The man grunted, "Is that the time then?"

I was confused, "I beg your pardon?"

"Is that the time then?" the man repeated and pointed a dirty finger towards the large, gilt, bracket clock on the wall behind me.

I turned and looked at the clock and stared at it for a moment or two. "Yes, it's half past ten."

"Then we must make haste, Watson!"

I turned back in shock! The fellow before me was laughing heartily and was removing the hat and a shaggy wig. I stood, my mouth opening and closing like that of a goldfish. "Holmes…great heavens! Why?"

Holmes had straightened up and was about to clap me on the back but remembered his dirty clothing. "It was necessary Watson. I needed to reconnoitre the place where I will meet Julia Moriarty and what better way than as a person with free access to all the nooks and crannies of a suburban railway station."

"A…a railway station?" I stammered

Holmes continued to shed the vestments of the railway worker. "Yes, I thought that the offer of meeting in a public place might somewhat reassure Madame Moriarty that this was rather less likely to be a trap. However, I need the help of brother Mycroft if I am to succeed."

Holmes retired to his room and some ten minutes later he returned as his old self. Pulling up a chair to the dining table, Holmes was immediately thoughtful. "I must pen my invitation with meticulous care, Watson. I want the lady to accept but her actions are to be under my control…without her ever knowing it. I think I must first have a meeting with Mycroft." At this, Holmes sprang from the table, gathered his coat and hastened down the

40

stairs. I have to say I was pleased that his wound was having little effect on his athleticism.

It was after lunch when Holmes returned. The smile on his face indicated to me that he was satisfied with the outcome of his meeting with Mycroft. "You seem extraordinarily pleased Holmes. What now?"

Holmes rubbed his hands together in anticipation. "Now it is time to offer the bait!" Holmes returned to the dining table and picked up his pen. He thought for perhaps thirty seconds and then began to write and, after a minute or so, he sat back. "Yes, I think that will do the trick. What do you think of this Watson?...'Madame Murphy, I wish to discuss with you the matters surrounding the death of your brother, James. I would be grateful if you could meet me tomorrow on the platform at Kennington underground railway station at precisely 4pm as I am travelling out of the city to an appointment in Stockwell. I would appreciate it if you were prompt as I will not wait. You have my word that I will travel alone and without protection. I trust you will do the same. Sherlock Holmes.'

I was mortified by what my friend had read out. "This cannot be Holmes. At least let me accompany you!"

Holmes shook his head. "No, Watson. This is something I must do alone. You may, however, accompany me to the station." I huffed and puffed but Holmes would hear none of it. He placed the note in an envelope, sealed it and rang for Mrs Hudson.

Chapter 9 - Madame Julia Moriarty

The following day, Holmes busied himself with meetings with Mycroft whilst I explored the history of London's underground railways. At 3pm we readied ourselves. "Are you sure that you will not take your revolver, Holmes?" I asked, knowing full well what the reply would be.

Holmes smiled confidently and patted me on the arm, "No, I cannot. I have given my word." We dressed warmly and hailed a cab to take us to Kennington Station.

As we travelled along, I began to consider Holmes's choice of location for the meeting. I had read that Kennington Station was part of the City of London & Southern Railway line. This was the first underground railway to have electric engines, a most agreeable improvement on the coal-fired locomotives. Indeed, the sulphurous stench from these engines had once been described by a person who had travelled in Africa as to being like 'the breath of an Alligator.'

The line runs from King William Street in the City, under the Thames and on to Stockwell in the suburbs, with the stations of Borough, Elephant and Castle, Kennington and The Oval between the two termini. I had travelled on this line several times and marvelled at the small electric engines that pulled three or four small carriages. Railway employees rode on each of the small platforms between the carriages. Here they operated the 'scissor' design gates and announced the name of the next station. It was interesting to note that the carriages had no windows save for some small strips of glass near the roof, the railway engineers arguing that there was nothing to be seen in the underground tunnels. However, the passengers soon named this rather claustrophobic design the 'padded cell'.

Soon we had reached the station and I feared greatly for my friend's safety. Holmes paid his two pence fare and passed through the turnstile. As he walked away towards the tiled tunnel of the station, he turned towards me and shouted, "I will meet you at Stockwell, Watson." and he waved farewell.

I was beside myself. My friend had gone alone and unarmed to meet a cold-blooded killer who would stop at nothing to avenge the death of her brother…and I was powerless! I could do little but trust that the superior intellect of my friend would prevail. I hailed a cab outside Kennington Station and made the seemingly endless journey to Stockwell. My heart was in my mouth as, upon my arrival, I saw a police van and an ambulance set off from outside the station at a fearsome pace.

There was a small group of people clustered round the station entrance. I pushed my way through to the turnstile only to have my path blocked by a burly constable. At my approach, the constable raised his hand, saying, "I'm sorry sir. I cannot let you onto the station; government orders."

I was incensed, "But…I must, my friend, Sherlock Holmes, I must find him!"

The constable shook his head, saying, "I'm sorry sir, he's not here. I've been here for a good hour and he hasn't passed me."

It felt as though my whole world had collapsed. Could it possibly be true that Julia Moriarty had triumphed and even now my friend was her captive or had she already avenged her brother? I was utterly despondent, there seemed to be nothing that I could do except return to Baker Street and wait for any news. In truth, I feared the worst.

Chapter 10 - Recounting the journey

The cab ride back to Baker Street seemed interminable but eventually I was once more back in our rooms. I immediately sought out Mrs Hudson but she had had no news of Holmes. I could not rest and must have paced for over half an hour before I heard footsteps on the stairs. I ran to our sitting room door and flung it open.

"Holmes!" I cried, and almost threw myself at him in relief. I embraced him, slapping him soundly several times on the back and only stopping when I remembered his wounds. Holmes had a pained expression on his face when I released him and I was immediately concerned, "Are you injured?"

Holmes smiled through the pain, "No, but I will thank you to not compress my ribs any further, Watson."

"What happened, Holmes? I waited at Stockwell and I feared the worst when I saw an ambulance leave the station at the gallop and you were nowhere to be seen."

Holmes crossed our sitting room to his old leather armchair and sat back. "Let me start at the point where I left you at the station turnstile. The platform had few passengers waiting for the 4pm train to Stockwell. As I waited, I looked around at my travelling companions but saw nobody of interest. The slight brush of air upon my face announced the train before it actually entered the station. It was then that a slim, female figure with flaming red hair stepped out from a niche in the tiled station wall and walked towards me. I noticed that she had her hand plunged deep inside her bag and, for a brief moment, I feared that she would shoot me out of hand…but no." I gasped and begged Holmes to continue.

The lady approached, saying, "Mr Holmes, I am on time and alone. I trust you are unarmed?" I opened my coat and jacket and she patted the pockets. Seeming satisfied, she withdrew her hand from her handbag and continued, "As I expected, you are an honourable man, even to your enemies…just like my brother."

I nodded my head, "Yes, I was most grateful that he allowed me to write a final note to Watson." Julia Moriarty gave a thin smile. The railway employee on the footplate of the nearest carriage had drawn back the 'scissor' style gate and I held out my arm. Julia Moriarty wagged her finger and refused it. Instead of going to the carriage that was nearest to me, she walked several yards to a carriage of her choice, one towards the rear. I smiled at her caution and again I offered my arm. This time she took it and we entered the carriage.

Inside the carriage, the seats were arranged longitudinally along its short length and there were already four people sitting there. I sat down beside Madame Moriarty and, as we waited for the train to move off, she opened her handbag to show me its contents. Within it I saw the glint of a nickel-plated, small calibre revolver.

As Julia Moriarty spoke, her voice turned to iron, "Please do not try to leave the carriage, Mr Holmes. I have so much more to discuss with you…but not here." I looked at her in a quizzical way. With a slight lurch, the train left the station. It was fascinating to see that, once the train was in motion, there was an immediate release of tension in her body. Perhaps now she believed herself to be in control. For the first time I looked fully into her face. She was undoubtedly an attractive woman, her age being perhaps a little more than 30 years. Her face was long and slightly oval, her fiercely auburn hair was tied back quite severely and she had piercing, bright blue eyes…but her expression was totally cold. Even at the thought of avenging her brother, her face showed little in the way of emotion.

After a few moments, she continued, "I am afraid that our train journey together will be shorter than you imagined for we will both leave the train at the next station. I shall leave the carriage first and then you will follow me. Should you choose to remain in the carriage, I have heavily armed associates on the platform ready to rake this carriage with gunfire and no-one, no-one, will survive…but of course, you will not let that happen."

I nodded sombrely, saying, "Of course."

She looked at me and gloated, "I regret that I will not be your companion to the terminus where, no doubt, you have a reception committee of your own waiting." For a moment, the slightest of smiles appeared on her face as I looked down towards the floor.

The train rolled on and then noticeably started to slow. The railway employee travelling on the footplate shouted out, "The Oval."

Julia Moriarty stood and turned to face me. "I am sure that I will enjoy our conversations over the last few days of your life, Mr Holmes…though I fear they may be excruciatingly painful for you." The train stopped. Julia Moriarty left the carriage and stepped down from the footplate. She walked a couple of paces onto the platform before turning and standing with her back towards the station wall. I stood looking out from the footplate. Behind her, beneath the station sign, I could see a group of heavily armed men in the shadows. She held out her gloved hand and beckoned me. "Come, Mr Holmes." I stepped down and walked slowly towards her. As I approached, she walked backwards until she stood within inches of the men in the shadows."

I think my eyes must have been like saucers as I urged Holmes to continue, "Go on! Go on!"

Holmes paused for a moment. "I have difficulty describing her expression as she was suddenly seized and disarmed by the police officers in plain clothes standing behind her.'

My pipe fell from my mouth and I scrabbled to retrieve it before it burned Mrs Hudson's carpet. "But…but how could you know…? What of her associates?"

Holmes held up his hand. "Have no fear, Watson. Julia Moriarty has been taken into custody, as have her associates at The Oval."

I thought back to my arrival at Stockwell. "So, the police van that I saw leaving Stockwell was probably carrying Madame Moriarty?"

Holmes nodded. "That is most likely. On my arrival at Stockwell, Mycroft immediately took me to the Station Master's office where he insisted that I recount to him what had occurred whilst a police constable took notes. I could see you standing at the turnstile but I could do nothing. By the time I was free to send a message, you had already departed. Mycroft required detailed answers and it is only now that he has released me."

I sat down, my mind still unable to comprehend what had happened. "But…but how was it achieved?"

Chapter 11 - The Grand Deception

Holmes smiled. "It was a grand deception, Watson. I knew that offering to meet her alone and unarmed in a public place would be just too much for her to resist. She knew me to be a man of my word and this meeting gave her what she thought to be an ideal opportunity to kidnap me and then dispose of me as she wished.

I chose Kennington for a good reason. There is only one stop between Kennington and the terminus at Stockwell. If Julia Moriarty wanted to remove me from the train, then it would be at The Oval where her associates would be lying in wait. I had to involve Mycroft. He replaced the railway staff travelling on the footplates between the carriages and those on the engine with his own men. You will recall, Watson, that the carriages have no windows and passengers rely on the railway staff to inform them of their arrival at the next station."

I thought for a moment. "Then the train passed through The Oval unannounced and went straight to Stockwell where Mycroft's men were waiting! Julia Moriarty believed she was alighting at The Oval!"

Holmes beamed. "Precisely, Watson!"

For a few moments I was elated...but then I began to consider the events. "Surely, Holmes, Julia

Moriarty has an intellect comparable to her brother's? She would have noticed the glow of the gaslights at The Oval station as the train passed through it and realised that she had been deceived!"

Holmes raised his forefinger. "Ah, for the deception to be a success, I had to call again on the influence of brother Mycroft. He arranged for the gaslights at The Oval Station to be dimmed to the same level as that of the tunnels shortly before the train passed through. Such action also provided Mycroft's men with the ideal opportunity to stealthily approach and capture her associates lying in wait, one of them being Silas Murchison."

I nodded as I considered this for a moment. "Yes, but what of the increase in journey time by travelling on to the next station? Would she not have realised…and…and what of the station sign on the platform? The sign for Stockwell Station must have been directly in front of her as she alighted from the train."

Holmes wagged his finger. "You must remember, Watson, that this is a person who has been incarcerated for some four years and is unfamiliar with journeys on the London underground railway. Other passengers in the carriage may have wondered but train speeds can vary and besides, I was the centre of her attention! I did, however, arrange a slight increase in the speed of the train and that shortened the journey time somewhat." Holmes paused for a moment and started to laugh. "As to the station sign...I have found that Her Majesty's printing works can produce some excellent signage at very short notice."

A few days later, Holmes's wounds had healed sufficiently to allow me to remove his stitches. Whilst he would always have a scar, there was no permanent damage. In the weeks that followed, we were kept abreast of affairs by regular bulletins from Mycroft, the last of these being that Julia Moriarty had been tried 'in camera.' As a result of a 'guilty' verdict, she was hanged, as a common murderer, under the name of Julia Murphy, together with Silas Murchison. The news of this brought no joy to Holmes. On reading it, he sat back and was silent for some considerable time.

A little later Holmes asked, "How do you view the year ahead, Watson?"

I thought for a moment. "Well, somewhat quieter I trust and I look forward to being able to see the rest of Mr Wilde's play without interruption!"

Holmes smiled at my reply and took a long draw on his pipe. "Yes, that is indeed something for us both to look forward to." Holmes was silent for a few moments more before saying, "I find many of Mr Wilde's quotations quite humorous but some, perhaps, to be a window on our world..."

'Our ambition should be to rule ourselves, the true kingdom for each one of us; and true progress is to know more, and be more, and to do more.'

After saying this he fell silent and we were both once again lost in our own thoughts.

Sherlock Holmes

-

The Highgate Magician

by Dick Gillman

Table of Contents

The Highgate Magician

Chapter 1 – 'The Great Borodino'

It was a pleasant afternoon at the beginning of June 1897 when Holmes and I first became acquainted with Mr James Carlisle Scott. A gentleman who was to be the catalyst for the case I have here recorded as that of 'The Highgate Magician'.

Holmes and I had just enjoyed a rather splendid cup of Darjeeling and were reaching for our pipes when Holmes edged forwards in his leather armchair, his head slightly to one side and was seen to be straining to hear something in the street below.

"What is it Holmes?" I enquired.

Holmes stood and pulled aside the net curtain to gain a better view of Baker Street and more particularly, the approach to the front door of 221b. He raised an eyebrow and his face bore a wry smile. "Ha! Here is a fellow with some purpose, Watson."

I stood and moved to the window. In the street below could be seen a rather rotund figure berating all about him and pushing his way through the throng of inhabitants of our metropolis who were going about their business. Apparently, in doing so, these poor souls were impeding this gentleman's progress to our door.

"It seems, Watson, that we are to have a visitor and one that is in exceedingly great haste to consult us."

At that moment, our doorbell was rung in a manner which I can only assume reflected the urgency of this gentleman's desire to seek us out. No sooner had the ringing ceased and the door had been answered than there could be plainly heard the thunder of feet upon the stairs as our visitor ascended. This was followed by the clatter of much lighter steps as Mrs Hudson followed in hot pursuit.

Within moments our sitting room door flew open and in burst a figure, clearly dishevelled and exhausted by his endeavours. Almost immediately the most disgruntled figure of Mrs Hudson was framed in the doorway.

Mrs Hudson's face was puce with both anger and exertion. "I'm sorry Mr Holmes, this 'gentleman' forced his way past me and ran up the stairs. Shall I call a constable?"

Holmes ran his expert eye over the figure of our visitor who was now standing, panting and supporting himself on the back of one of our dining chairs.

"No, no... that will not be necessary, Mrs Hudson, I do not think we are in any danger…either real or imagined."

At this, I saw the expression on the man's face change to one of surprise. It was for a moment as if Holmes had said something that had resonated with our guest in an unexpected way.

Mrs Hudson gave our visitor a hard stare, saying, "Very well, sir." She straightened and smoothed her apron with both hands before tossing her head and leaving our rooms.

Holmes smiled and turned his attention to our visitor. "Now sir, if you would be so kind as to take a seat and tell us how we may be of service."

We both sat and the man before us moved a newspaper from a fireside chair before sitting, facing us. Pulling out a large, red, cotton handkerchief, he mopped his brow before launching forth in a manner which, whilst not a tirade, was certainly very forthright in its tone.

"Mr Holmes, I have to say from the outset that I am a man not used to seeking out private detectives for I am of the opinion that they inhabit a world to which I am no stranger. However, you have come highly recommended and I am prepared to ask for your help."

I must admit that I was appalled at the arrogance of this fellow and was just about to rise from my chair and tell him so when Holmes placed a hand on my arm; a wry smile had spread across his face. I sat back and looked quizzically at Holmes as he drew up his knees and placed his forefinger against his lips.

Holmes smiled at our guest. "Ah, yes! You are indeed wise to question the methods of detection for they can appear to be magical to those untrained in their arts."

Again I saw the expression on our guest's face change for it now took on a look of both surprise and something perhaps akin to mistrust.

Holmes continued, "Please forgive me for I have not introduced my colleague. This is my friend, Dr John Watson. Watson, allow me to introduce 'The Great Borodino'."

As I looked across at our visitor, his jaw dropped and I thought his eyes might truly pop from his head. "But…but…that is impossible!" he stammered.

Holmes smiled broadly and wagged his forefinger. "Not so, sir…for there is more. You live in Highgate, you are unmarried and at present you do not have the funds to employ a maid. You make little money from your career as a stage magician despite currently performing daily at The Middlesex Music Hall. You have very recently had an accident

60

to your right hand and this causes you to now shave using an American safety razor."

Our guest just sat with his mouth opening and closing with no intelligible sounds coming from him. Indeed, I initially thought he had had a seizure but after a few moments he managed to weakly splutter, "How?"

Holmes began to fill his pipe. "I will explain my methods and afterwards, sir, you might like to revise your opinion of those who practise the skills of detection? I do not believe in magic and have been known to expose charlatans whose sole purpose is to prey on the weak and gullible. However, those who openly use the skills of deception and misdirection for the purpose of entertainment are quite a different matter."

Our guest nodded and once again mopped his brow, saying, "I apologise if I have offended you Mr Holmes, it was certainly not my intention."

Satisfied by the sincerity of our visitor, Holmes began his discourse. "When you swept into our rooms, I noticed that the interior of your cloak displayed a series of striking geometric patterns. I determined that the pattern was to disguise the concealed pockets I had observed, pockets that are required for your employment. This informed me that you were either a stage magician or a pickpocket. Clearly not the latter!"

Our guest smiled for the first time and I saw him begin to visibly relax.

Holmes continued, "Having established your occupation and that you had arrived in Baker Street in your stage clothes, I determined that the theatre where you were appearing must be within a reasonable walking distance. Travelling on foot also had the benefit of saving the cab fare."

I looked across at our visitor and he was nodding his head, obviously intrigued.

Holmes blew out a thin stream of blue tobacco smoke before continuing, "I observed from our window that you came north up Baker Street. The only theatre within walking distance to the south that has a matinee featuring a magician is The Middlesex Music Hall. This establishment boasts the appearance of 'The Great Borodino.' Your clothes are of good quality but are well worn which also tells me you have limited funds at present. I saw your fingernails and they clearly bore the evidence of coal dust beneath them. This indicates to me that you cannot afford a maid as you had had to lay the fire yourself this morning. Your collar and shirt, whilst neat, had not been ironed perfectly. If you had been married, your wife would have no doubt ensured that you were turned out immaculately."

Holmes pulled on his pipe and inclined his head slightly as he took another incisive look at our visitor, as if to confirm his appraisal. "You are clean-shaven but your face shows some small razor cuts. I observed, when you moved the newspaper from the chair, that you were right handed. Surely a man who has prodigious sleight of hand skills would not be inept in the use of a razor? Using a cut-throat razor in your left hand would be both dangerous and impractical so the solution is a safety razor. This implies some recent damage to your right hand. Finally, as to the location of your home, I noticed a return ticket stub protruding from your waistcoat pocket upon which could be seen the first three letters: 'Hig-.' From its colour, it could only be a tram ticket from Highgate."

I have to admit I was enjoying this masterful display of observation and deduction from Holmes… and in truth, so was our guest.

Chapter 2 – The vanishing assistant

Our guest was clearly impressed by Holmes's skills and when he spoke, he appeared to be rather humbled. "Mr Holmes, I sit before you in amazement. I am in awe of your powers of observation and deduction. I come to you because of an occurrence that I cannot explain or rationalise. My given name is James Carlisle Scott and as you correctly determined, I perform as a stage magician under the name 'The Great Borodino'. My mother was Russian and the name is some small link to my heritage. I have been appearing at The Middlesex Music Hall for one week for the matinee performance. I employ my niece, Emily Scott, as my on-stage assistant. She is my brother's child and hopes one day to take to the stage herself as she has an excellent singing voice."

Holmes nodded and encouraged Scott to continue.

Scott's voice took on a more serious note, "It is of her disappearance that I wish to consult you as it happened in a most curious way. The preparations for this afternoon's performance seemed to be proceeding as normal. I was in my dressing room finishing my makeup. It was taking a little longer than usual after my mishap earlier in the week with a fire door which trapped and severely bruised my right hand. My niece had gone onto the stage to ensure that all the props for our act were present and in the correct positions.

The curtain went up and my performance began as usual but I could see from her expression that Emily was in some way a little troubled. There was nothing I could do mid-performance and so we continued with the act. The finale is the 'Mysterious Vanishing Lady' where Emily walks inside the box and I close the door. With a wave and a tap of my wand she disappears, to the amazement of the audience. Then, with another wave of the wand, she re-appears…only on this occasion she did not! I opened the box and she had truly disappeared! The audience saw my look of disbelief and of course was entertained by it, thinking it to be part of the act. But Mr Holmes, when the curtains closed, she was still missing. I hunted for her and then informed the stage manager. The theatre was searched but there was no sign of her either above or below stage. She has truly vanished and I am at my wits end!"

It was plain that he was genuinely distressed; he hid his face in his hands and began to sob, "Please, Mr Holmes, I beg you, find Emily. My brother entrusted her to me and now she has vanished. It may perhaps seem an ironic situation but I have a grave responsibility for her welfare."

I looked across at Holmes. He was sitting back in his chair and had a thoughtful look upon his face. "Tell me, Mr Scott, how is the final trick performed?"

Scott leaned forwards. "It is a simple trick, Mr Holmes. The box has no floor and it sits exactly over a hydraulic trap door in the stage. Once Emily has entered the box, I tap upon it with my wand and this is the signal for a stagehand in the wings to operate the trap door. This in turn lowers Emily below the level of the stage and after a few moments, I open the box to reveal her disappearance. When I tap upon the box for a second time, the stagehand again operates the trap and Emily is raised and returned to the box."

Holmes blew out a thin stream of blue smoke. "Is there anyone below the stage to receive Emily?"

Scott thought for a moment, "No, Mr Holmes. There is no need."

Holmes frowned briefly. "I am reticent to ask this but has your niece ever done anything like this before? Has she shown any signs of a romantic interest and might she, perhaps, have run off?"

Scott looked shocked. "No sir! Never! Emily is a good girl. She is happy in her work and has no reason to stray."

On hearing this, I noticed a grim look pass briefly across Holmes's face. "I think then that we need to accompany you back to the theatre and examine the stage and its workings." With that, Holmes rose, tapped his pipe out into the fire grate and walked to collect his hat and coat.

Scott remained seated, shocked perhaps by the pace of events. "You…you will take the case, Mr Holmes?" he stammered.

Holmes looked serious. "Indeed, Mr Scott. I am gravely concerned for your niece's welfare and I need to examine the scene of her disappearance as soon as possible."

Gathering our coats, Holmes and I ushered our new client down the stairs and out into Baker Street. Holmes flagged down a passing four-wheeler and we were soon on our way. I thought I might ask Scott who else was appearing at the theatre. "Tell me, Mr Scott, are you top of the bill at the theatre?"

At this, Scott laughed quietly. "Oh no, indeed not Dr Watson. I am only retained for the afternoon matinee; there are several nationally known acts appearing in the evening performance. There is even an international pianist on tomorrow evening's bill, all the way from Germany, a Herr Johann Richter."

Holmes leant forwards, "Richter, you say! I have read of this fellow. He is not a pianist by profession, he is an advisor and close confident of the Kaiser. However, his ego is such that he plays to an audience whenever he has the opportunity. I had read that he was in Britain and he is indeed a fine pianist but his choice of pieces is, perhaps, a little too Prussian for my musical tastes. My brother Mycroft might be more interested than I."

Chapter 3 – The search for Emily

In a few minutes we arrived outside the grand façade of the theatre although we were to see little of it. Our client quickly hustled us down a passage at the side of the building which led to the stage door set in the drab, red brick wall. To one side was a window through which could be seen a plainly bored clerk who was sitting reading a newspaper.

Our client led the way through the stage door and into a small vestibule within which there was an office door and a small, open window. "Good afternoon Tom. Is there any news of Emily?"

The clerk looked up from his newspaper and shook his head saying, "I'm sorry, Mr Scott, there is no sign of her." I looked at James Scott and believe that I saw his shoulders slump even lower at this news.

Below the window was a small, green painted shelf screwed to the wall and upon it were a pencil attached to an eyelet in the wall by a piece of string and a visitor's book. The clerk's job seemed to be to take messages and to sign visitors in and out. A single glance at the visitor's book showed that the clerk carried out his duties in an unacceptably lax manner. Many of the entries were simply a signature consisting of unintelligible scribble and the entry and exit times were, for the most part, left blank.

Scott led the way through the internal passageways of the theatre towards the stage. I had seen on the billboard for the evening performance that there was to be a series of burlesque, music hall acts. Stagehands could be seen busily moving and positioning large, garishly painted canvas 'flats' and erecting a podium from which the 'Master of Ceremonies' would preside with his gavel.

Holmes roved the stage with our client and soon he had located the precise position on the stage where the magic box had stood. Looking down, I noticed that upon the stage there had been painted lines, circles, squares and rectangles, each one numbered and relating to the positions for various props and items of scenery. The position for the magic box was marked by a square outline in pale yellow paint. This also delineated the edges of the trap door. Holmes was soon on his hands and knees and examining intently the surface of the trapdoor with his glass. As I watched, I noticed him glance across at me and nod slightly. His face was grim.

Holmes stood up and dusted the knees of his trousers. "Mr Scott, I wonder if you might show Dr Watson your niece's dressing room. There may be some small clue there that might help us."

Scott nodded, "Certainly, Mr Holmes. This way Dr Watson."

I left the stage with a heavy heart for I knew that the nod from Holmes meant that he had found something of importance. He now wanted me to be some small distraction whilst he continued his investigations.

Scott lead me through several narrow passageways until we came to a row of plain wooden doors, each with a small card held in place by a tack. Upon the one in front of us was scrawled the name 'Emily Scott.' Our client knocked, seemingly hoping against hope for a reply…but there was none. He opened the door and we entered the tiny dressing room. The room was quite well lit, a necessity for applying the stage makeup used by all the performers. Clothes were neatly arranged on hangers and a small leather suitcase had been pushed into the kneehole beneath the mirror. A naked electric light bulb either side of the mirror provided light which was harsh but adequate for the task.

"Is that your niece's suitcase?" I asked, pointing towards the kneehole.

Scott looked down and squinted into the shadows. "Yes, yes, I believe it is."

"Would you have any objections if..?" I let the question hang for a moment.

Reaching down, Scott retrieved the case and laid it upon the table top beneath the mirror. It was clear from his expression that he did not wish to pry but he was aware of its potential to supply some insight into his niece's disappearance. I allowed him to open the case which was not locked. It held a small amount of clothing, a hairbrush, comb and some hair ornaments. There was nothing to suggest that she was about to go on a journey. I noticed that, tucked in the bottom of the case, there were three or four envelopes that had been tied into a small bundle with pink ribbon. Again I looked questioningly at Scott and with a face filled with great sadness, he nodded.

With very great care I took the bundle and undid the ribbon, placing it carefully back into the case. The first one was unsealed but had been stamped ready for posting. It was addressed to a 'Mr and Mrs E Scott' with an address in Brighton.

I read aloud to Scott. "Dearest Papa and Mama, I am having such great fun here in London with Uncle James and I am learning so very much about the theatre. Our performances have been so well received that my confidence is growing daily. I truly hope that by the end of our tour, I will be ready to step out onto the stage myself…" and so it continued. It was a joyous letter to loving parents with no hint of any clouds on the horizon. The other letters were from Emily's parents and addressed to her in Highgate. They too were gentle and full of family news, equally jolly and full of encouragement.

After I had finished, I turned and saw that Scott was holding his handkerchief to his eyes and, in truth, I too was moved, even more so as I again recalled the grim look that Holmes had given me a few minutes earlier.

It was as I retied the little bundle of letters that there was a slight knock at the dressing room door and a pageboy appeared. "Please sir, Mr Holmes wants Dr Watson to follow me and there is a Police Inspector at the stage door for Mr Scott."

Scott jolted out of his melancholy and rushed away hoping for news of his niece. I followed the page who led me to a staircase that descended beneath the stage. The page pointed down the stairs saying, "He's down there sir. He said to leave you here and you would make your own way." I gave the lad a sixpence and began to make my way carefully downward, step-by-step, beneath the stage.

At the foot of the flight of stairs I could see that the void was lit by strings of fairly dim electric lights, each bulb producing a small pool of light. Outside this pool there was a considerable amount of darkness. The trusses supporting the stage sprouted upwards and outwards at head height, rather like the canopies of several large trees which seemed to march away into the distance, so vast was the stage.

"Holmes!" I cried.

To my relief, I heard an answering voice calling, "Over here, Watson…and have a care with your head!"

The voice had come from some distance away and in an area where there was but little light. Holmes called again and at once I was sharply reminded of the presence of extensive carpentry when I turned towards his voice and received a glancing blow to the side of my head. Cursing myself, I made my way towards him.

As I drew near, I could see Holmes's familiar crouching silhouette but beside him I saw a ragged bundle. I looked down and before I could stop myself, blurted out, "Lord! No!"

There, beside Holmes, was the body of a slight, young woman. In the dim light I could see the weak sparkle from the sequins sewn onto her costume. "How did she die, Holmes?"

Holmes moved slightly to one side and there I could see the pool of blood that had poured from her body. Her head was to one side and this revealed a single, slim cut that had neatly severed the windpipe, carotid and jugular.

Holmes's voice was ice cold, "I noticed when we were on the stage that the surface of the trapdoor showed signs of a struggle but it was some time before I discovered her body. The light is so poor down here and it had been hidden beneath a pile of canvas. This killing was not a simple crime of passion nor a robbery. This was a deliberate execution, Watson."

I gasped, "But she was a gentle little thing. What harm had she done?"

Holmes paused for a moment. "I do not know, but in her final seconds she has left us a clue. In her dying moments, she was laid on an old, oil-painted theatre canvas. Using her own blood, she has written this." Holmes struck a match and in its light I could see the girl's bloodied hand. At her fingertip was written the word 'PAIN' with her outstretched index finger pointing to the word and leaving a bloody mark next to the letter 'N'.

In my many years as a physician I had seldom seen such a moving scene. "My Lord! What an epitaph: 'pain'…but why write 'pain'? How is this a clue?"

The light from the match flickered briefly as it expired and I could no longer see Holmes's face. From the darkness his voice replied, "I am unsure… but I have something of an idea. It is imperative that Scott should not see her body like this. I called for the police as soon as I discovered her body. They will occupy him for a little while. Given the circumstances of Emily's death, I have advised them to tell him something a little short of the whole truth. Come Watson, I require some time to consider the facts. We must return to Baker Street."

I nodded and we slowly and carefully made our way beneath the stage and back to the stairs. At the stage door Scott could be seen in the clerk's office. His head was in his hands and his body heaved as he softly wept. I was about to open the office door but a hand on my sleeve guided me away and off towards the street.

Chapter 4 – A little practical Chemistry

Nothing was said in the short cab ride back to Baker Street, each of us was deep in our own thoughts and each grateful to be left without the intrusion of the other. Once inside, we sat in silence for perhaps twenty minutes, our drawing room attaining that intense blue haze from copious amounts of tobacco smoke.

It was Holmes who was first to break the silence. Taking his pipe from his mouth, he pointed the stem towards me, "Tell me Watson, if you were to die like that young woman, what would you write as your last word?"

I thought for several moments. "Why, I would write the name of my killer, if it were known to me."

Holmes tapped the stem of his pipe against his hand. "Yes… as would I, but I believe that the person who killed her was a professional who grasped his victim from behind and remained unseen. What then? Might I suggest the word to be a clue as to **why** she was killed…but why write 'pain'? Clearly pain was something that she felt and her hand was seen to be pointing to it…unless… unless the word was unfinished!"

I sat upright in my chair. "What? There was to be more? I think it unlikely, in the few seconds that she had, that she could have written a second word."

Holmes nodded slowly. "Precisely Watson. It was a single word but unfinished. Her finger was not pointing to the word; she was trying to complete it. 'PAINT' is the only logical answer…but for the moment I am at a loss as to its significance."

I sat back in my chair, my brain still struggling to take in the horrors of the day and now this. We continued to sit in silence until late into the evening. Supper was eaten and, in truth, I looked forward to seeing the morning and a new day.

The following morning I found that Holmes had risen early and had breakfasted alone. He was seated in his armchair and was now engrossed in reading 'The Times'.

"Good morning Holmes. I had a wretched night. I trust you are more refreshed than I." The only response I received was a grunt from behind the newspaper. I rang the bell and was soon tucking in to two boiled eggs and bread and butter. This was followed by toast and a generous helping of Seville marmalade. After ten minutes my curiosity got the better of me. "What is it that you find so fascinating in 'The Times', Holmes?"

Holmes placed the newspaper in his lap and sat back with a frown upon his face. "It is the possible international aspect of this case that is gnawing at me Watson. I hesitate to look in that direction but it is that that draws my attention."

I was perplexed. "International aspect? You mean that German pianist fellow that is to perform at the theatre this evening?" I enquired.

Folding the paper, Holmes tossed it to one side. "Hmm, I cannot but think of this fellow's political connections. Though meant in jest, when I suggested that Mycroft might be interested in Herr Richter, I now have the feeling that I may have been subconsciously not far from the mark."

I was once more confused. "Mycroft? Are you sure? But why?"

Holmes rose and began to pace, a clear sign that he was turning over ideas and considering countless possibilities in that colossus that was his mind. Suddenly he stopped pacing and a thin smile appeared upon his lips. "I think that it is time to float a fly down the Thames and see who comes up to bite." With that, Holmes reached for his notebook and silver pencil, dashing off a telegram before ringing the bell for Mrs Hudson.

It was some ten minutes later, as we were sitting at our ease, when there was a frenzied ringing of our front door bell. Holmes was immediately alert and listened attentively whilst Mrs Hudson conversed with our caller. A few moments later we heard the familiar tread on the stairs of the lady herself followed by a knock on our door.

Mrs Hudson crossed the room and proffered an envelope to Holmes. "Mr Holmes, a constable left this note for you. He said it was urgent."

Holmes leapt from his chair, reached for the envelope and tore it open. I could see from his expression that he was greatly concerned. "There has been another death at the theatre, Watson. This time it is one of the stagehands. We must make haste." Rushing to the coat stand, Holmes grabbed his cloak and hat and was gone with me trailing in his wake.

A Hansom was hailed and soon we were speeding south along Baker Street before turning east towards the theatre. I had recovered from my dash downstairs and race towards the cab and now had sufficient breath to ask a question, "Is it another murder, Holmes?"

Holmes face was set in stone. "It is not clear from the note. It simply says that the stagehand died a mysterious death from a creeping paralysis."

I pondered this in silence. My initial thought was poison but I kept my own counsel. Soon we were at the theatre and once again at the stage door. A constable was standing guard and saluted at our approach. Once inside we were met by an Inspector Warren who swiftly showed us into a washroom to one side of the main corridor. A table had been brought in, upon which a body had been placed and covered with a dustsheet. The inspector leaned close to Holmes, saying, "This is Bill Bradley, he'd worked here as a stagehand for over twenty years."

Holmes nodded and removed the sheet. Beneath it could be seen the body of a man of approximately fifty years. His clothes were those of a manual labourer: hobnail boots, well-worn trousers with a wide belt, a striped shirt and a waistcoat. Around his neck was a sweat cloth and by his side had been placed a somewhat grimy flat cap. I watched closely as Holmes examined the body. When he reached the man's hands, I saw him pay particular attention to the fingers. Holmes passed me his glass, asking, "What do you make of this, Watson?"

I looked closely at the man's fingers. Although heavily calloused, the skin looked raw on the fingertips but not on the pad of the thumb, only on the lower side closest to the palm. "It appears to be some kind of burn, as though he has rested both hands on something caustic. It is a chemical burn rather than one from a source of heat. However, I fail to see how this could have caused death."

Holmes nodded. "Yes, quite so." He turned to the Inspector, asking, "Are you aware of any caustic substances on the premises Inspector?"

The Inspector paused, "None that I am aware of, Mr Holmes, but some strong cleaning products are used here and part of this man's duties was that of a cleaner."

Holmes frowned for a moment. "Inspector, would you be so kind as to ask one of your constables to bring me a bar of soap, a piece of blotting paper and a glass of red wine?"

Inspector Warren eyed Holmes warily and rubbed his chin, saying, "I hardly think that this is an appropriate time to be drinking alcohol, Mr Holmes."

A wry smile spread across Holmes's face. "Please humour me in this, Inspector. It may be very important."

The Inspector did not appear to be convinced but dispatched one of his constables to fetch what Holmes had requested. Within five minutes there was a knock at the door and a constable placed the three items on the table.

Holmes rubbed his hands. "Now gentlemen, let us embark on a little chemistry." Holmes tore from the blotting paper two thin strips approximately a quarter of an inch wide and dipped each of them in the red wine. "This is to be our very simple Litmus paper so let us begin with the soap. I moisten the bar with a little water from the tap and let a drop of the liquid touch the wine-soaked blotting paper." As we watched, the first wine-soaked blotting paper strip changed colour from red to a strong blue.

Smiling, Holmes continued, "This is our alkaline colour, let us then test the victim's burns." Holmes repeated the test, placing the second piece of blotting paper on the dead man's fingertips. This time the colour remained red. "So, gentlemen, our simple test eliminates any strong alkaline cleaning product. Whilst both acidic and neutral substances do not cause the wine to change colour, a neutral substance could not be responsible for such skin damage. Therefore, I suggest we need to look for a strongly acidic substance… and I very much doubt that there is a store of such within the theatre!"

The Inspector was clearly intrigued. "So, you believe that the acid had been brought into the theatre and somehow the victim has placed his hands upon a surface treated with acid?"

Holmes nodded. "Exactly, but why and how remains, for the moment, a mystery…and we are no nearer finding the cause of death. Was this man working alone when he became ill, Inspector?"

Inspector Warren shook his head. "No sir. He was working with another man, Harry Small. I have interviewed him but I admit I obtained little information of any value from him. Would you care to speak to him?"

Holmes looked around him, saying, "Yes, I would be most obliged, Inspector…but not here, I think."

Chapter 5 – The Bechstein

Inspector Warren led the way across the passage to a small office where a man of a similar age to that of the victim was sitting. The man rose as we entered but Holmes motioned him to be seated. Holmes smiled. "Mr Small, you were working with Mr Bradley when he died?"

Harry Small had removed his cap and was wringing it between his hands. "Yes sir. We was shifting stuff around ready for the performance tonight. There were flats to move and backdrops. The stage had to be cleared, all by hand. We had just moved some stuff when Bill says, 'My hands are burning,' and I laughed. I thought he had chafed them on some rope as we had hauled up some of the flysheets. Anyways, he keeps complaining and then, as we were moving some boxes, he drops one. I blames him something rotten but he says he can't feel his hands and then slowly his arms goes dead and…and then he has trouble breathing and then he just dies on me! I ain't ever seen anything like it."

I looked at Harry Small and he was trembling like a leaf. I patted him on the shoulder, saying, "Thank you Mr Small. You have been most helpful."

Just as we were about to leave, Holmes turned and asked, "By the by, Mr Small, has there been any scenery painting done over the last day or so?"

Harry Small was silent for a moment. "Why, no sir. We only repaints when there is to be a new production and that won't be until next week." Holmes smiled, nodded in thanks and we left the office.

As we stood in the passageway, Holmes turned to me, asking quietly, "Well, Watson, what are your thoughts on the cause of death?"

This was something I had already considered. "I am of the opinion that he was killed by a chemical toxin that entered his body through his wounds. It was seen to spread quickly from there, causing paralysis. This suggests to me the possibility of a muscle or nerve poison."

Holmes nodded. "Yes, I agree. I think it is time for us to look around once more on the stage." Nodding to the Inspector, we made our way through the wings to the now brightly lit stage. The stage manager could be seen directing his staff to move flats into position. A backdrop consisting of a large, ornate velvet curtain had been lowered in order to give the stage a more elegant appearance, in keeping with an evening of classical music.

Holmes paused briefly to examine each of the flats at the side of the stage. "It is as Mr Small said, these canvases have not been painted for some time."

I did notice, however, that when Holmes examined the flats, he had put on his black leather gloves as a precaution.

In the centre of the stage there had now been placed a very fine grand piano and stool. The cover of the keyboard was down, as was the lid, and as we approached, I could see the maker's name gleaming in gold lettering: 'Bechstein.'

Holmes was drawn to the piano as a moth is to a candle flame. He caressed its surface with his gloved hand whilst saying, "Ah, a fine example from Bechstein Pianofortefabrik. From its age, it is likely to have been made in their Berlin factory." Carefully, Holmes lifted the cover of the keyboard and played a few notes. Looking about him, Holmes pulled out the piano stool and removed his gloves. With a twinkle in his eye, Holmes flexed and stretched his fingers saying, "I have always had a desire to play a grand piano on stage, Watson."

At the very moment that he was about to play, an angry bellow of "Halt! Stop!" made Holmes pause. Across the apron of the stage, the figure of a large and obviously very angry man rushed towards us. In German, and very strongly accented English, the man continued to shout at us. "Gott in Himmel! What the do you think you are doing? This is my piano and I am the only one who plays it. I bring it with me from Germany!" With that, he slammed the keyboard cover firmly shut. "Who are you?"

Holmes stood up and bowed slightly. "I am sorry if I have offended you, Herr Richter. I was not aware that this was your personal piano. I am Sherlock Holmes and this is Dr Watson."

I nodded towards the man who was clearly still seething with anger.

Richter continued to bellow, "Holmes? Holmes? The only man of this name that I know works in your Whitehall. What are you doing here?"

I was just about to speak when Holmes raised his hand slightly. "We are here to investigate the disappearance of Emily Scott. Are you aware of this?"

Herr Richter moved closer and looked Holmes directly in the eye. "I have heard something of it but it has nothing to do with me or my piano. Please leave! At once!"

Holmes nodded, saying "Thank you Herr Richter. I look forward to your performance this evening." With that, Holmes turned on his heel and strode away leaving me to simply nod and follow.

As we walked back through the theatre towards the stage door, I felt the need to raise this fellow's rudeness with Holmes. "I think that was rather uncalled for, Holmes. The man seems obsessed with his piano!"

A smile passed over Holmes's face and he wagged his finger in my direction. "Ah, but perhaps I would be just as protective of my beloved Stradivarius if some stranger were to come to our rooms and simply pick it up and play it. Remember, Watson, the man is a Prussian."

In truth it was a parallel that I had not even considered. "Yes, yes, I can see the similarity…though I thought his reaction to be a little harsh. It was interesting, however, that he knew Mycroft."

Holmes's pace slowed. "Yes, that took me somewhat by surprise. I had at that precise moment seen the man purely as a musician rather than as a person of some very considerable power and influence within the Kaiser's circle of confidants. It will be of some interest to see whether my telegram to Mycroft has produced results."

Leaving the theatre we swiftly hailed a cab and travelled back to Baker Street. Even as we opened the front door, Mrs Hudson appeared clutching an envelope. "This is for you, Mr Holmes. It came by Government messenger with the instruction for you to open it immediately on your return."

Holmes turned and looked at me, a wicked glint in his eye. "Thank you Mrs Hudson. Come, Watson, let us see what intelligence brother Mycroft needs to convey so urgently."

Once safely in our rooms, Holmes opened the envelope and read the note within. "Well, well, well, Watson. We appear to have stirred up a veritable Hornet's nest. My telegram to Mycroft stated that we were investigating a murder and that we intended to speak to a Herr Richter."

This information caught me off guard and I spluttered…"But we weren't!"

Holmes had now a serious note to his voice, "No, but it seems that Her Majesty's government has some particular interest in Herr Richter and wants us to stay well clear of him. The reply from Mycroft only makes me more certain that there is more to this case than I first imagined."

Holmes tossed me the note from Mycroft which read thus, 'Sherlock, on no account must you make contact with Richter. He has diplomatic status and, as such, is inviolate. You will cease your investigation immediately. Should it come to my attention that you have not, you will be arrested under the Official Secrets Act and held until I deem it safe for you to be released. Mycroft.'

Whilst I did not fully comprehend what was afoot, I was incensed! "You are being threatened by your own brother with what amounts to indefinite incarceration for simply talking to a man? This is outrageous!"

Holmes appeared thoughtful and sat back in his chair with his eyes closed and his fingers steepled against his lips. "It is those last few words that I find so interesting, Watson, '…until I deem it **safe** for you to be released.' It is the aspect of safety that intrigues me. Mycroft is keeping me safe…but from what or from whom? What is to happen? Is Richter in danger and if so, from whom..? Unless…unless…"

Suddenly Holmes sprang upright. "No! It cannot be possible! It is imperative that I summon Mycroft here to explain himself!" With that Holmes scrabbled for his notebook and wrote two words upon a page, hastily folded it and rang furiously for Mrs Hudson.

Chapter 6 – Unwelcome news

It was about an hour later that our doorbell rang. Holmes had been pacing madly for the previous fifteen minutes and had it continued, I would have indeed feared for his sanity. At the sound of the doorbell, he stopped and gathered himself together whilst our visitor climbed the stairs. The door to our rooms opened and in walked Mycroft Holmes.

Holmes was shaking with anger. He could barely contain himself, "Tell me that she no longer lives." Mycroft simply stood, rooted to the spot. Holmes now raged, "Tell me Mycroft, upon your honour, is she alive?"

I looked from one brother to the other, unsure as to what I was witnessing. Mycroft gave a brief nod. This reply turned Sherlock into a silent, seething cauldron of hatred, something I had never seen before.

In an icy voice, filled with malice, Sherlock asked, "Why? For God's sake, why?"

Mycroft stumbled and I thought he might fall but he walked somehow to a chair. He seemed to find it difficult to look at his brother and his only reply was, "Necessity."

At this Sherlock laughed manically, "Necessity! Necessity, you say? I take it that the Crown's needs override justice?"

Mycroft could still not face his brother. "It was not my doing, Sherlock. I argued vehemently against it, even to the point where I was accused of being influenced by my feelings for my brother. Had I continued to press the point, I would have been removed from my position. Whilst I have some power within the government, I cannot override the decisions of the Prime Minister and the Cabinet."

Up until this point I was in a fog and then suddenly I realised that they were talking of Julia Moriarty! "But...but... she was hanged. We had a written note from you, Mycroft!"

Mycroft shook his head. "I wrote what I was told to write. She lives."

Holmes had now quietened a little. "What did she offer the government?"

Mycroft sat back in his chair. "I think it would be better if I were to tell all. Once Julia Moriarty had been captured and the death sentence pronounced, a very senior member of the bar, a Queen's Counsel acting as an intermediary, approached the Prime Minister. This intermediary informed him that Julia Moriarty had access to secret documents from within the Kaiser's own office. They related to the expansion plans of Germany in Africa and also the plans for the expansion of the German Naval fleet."

Holmes had now retired to his old leather armchair and had his knees pulled up tightly to his chest.

Mycroft continued, "Her Majesty's government deemed this information to be priceless. As a sign of good faith, Julia Moriarty's intermediary delivered a sample of the documents to the government. The War Office was ecstatic. This was exactly the information that they had been trying to acquire for months and had little chance of obtaining. The government was convinced and was willing to secretly release her. There was little difficulty in this. She had been tried 'in camera' so the public was none the wiser. However, the War Office made one proviso…"

Holmes unfolded his legs and leant forwards in his chair. There was now no colour in his face and his expression was of carved marble. "Allow me to guess, dear brother. Her Majesty's government wanted Julia Moriarty's organisation to carry out one small task for them…to kill Johann Richter."

Mycroft nodded slowly. "He is a very powerful man with huge influence within the 'Flottenverein', the Navy League. He has influence over a million members. He also has the backing of the major armaments and steel companies and he has the Kaiser's ear. Even more importantly, he is rumoured to be the draftsman elect of a new Navy Bill designed to greatly expand the German Imperial Navy, the Kaiserliche Marine."

Holmes rose from his chair and again started to pace. "How was this assassination to be carried out, Mycroft?"

Mycroft shook his head. "In truth, I do not know. The only stipulation of the government was that it was to be done quietly."

Stopping in front of Mycroft, Holmes posed a question, "What then if I were to tell you that I believe that he is to be killed tonight before a crowd of several hundred people?"

A look of horror and disbelief passed across Mycroft's face. "No, that is not possible. It is not…"

"What? Part of the deal? When was Julia Moriarty released?" queried Holmes.

Mycroft nodded, adding, "She was released a month ago as our part of the bargain after having furnished all the papers as promised. We were informed that it was necessary for her to be free in order to make the arrangements. You must understand, Sherlock, I am not privy to the details."

Sherlock Holmes began to pace again, saying, "Were you aware that these 'arrangements' included the murder of an innocent young girl?"

Mycroft gasped and turned his head swiftly towards Sherlock, "What?"

"You may well ask, but you have released the genie from the bottle Mycroft. There are no boundaries to Moriarty's wickedness. My client's niece was a sweet, innocent child. It is my belief that she saw something yesterday that cost her her life. The assassin must also have seen her but could not act before she went on stage. She would no doubt tell someone of what she had seen and then the game would be up. He had to silence her quickly and he did so during the finale of the act."

Mycroft's face was ashen. He softly said, "I am truly sorry, Sherlock. This was not meant to be."

Sherlock did not look at his brother. He simply reached for his hat and coat, saying, "I am going to the theatre to try and save the life of a man who has done nothing wrong save to ably serve his country. We are not yet at war Mycroft. Julia Moriarty has planned to supremely embarrass the British Government. Imagine the headlines tomorrow when she exposes their involvement in such a public assassination. I fear that if she succeeds, war may be very much closer than you might think!"

With that, Holmes made his way down the stairs and I quickly followed.

Chapter 7 – The deadly solution

Together, and in silence, we took a cab to the theatre. The stage door was now quiet and the evening's entertainment was to start barely ten minutes after our arrival. Once again we made our way towards the side of the stage and were pleased to again meet Harry Small, the stagehand. Looking onto the stage I could see that Herr Richter's grand piano had now been placed centre stage. Holmes was alert, constantly looking around him like some garden bird, ever wary of his surroundings.

Harry Small was standing by the large winding handle for the curtains. As I stood by his side, he let out a large sigh, saying, "Bill would have loved this, you know. We used to go out of an evening, as two couples, to the 'Victoria Hotel' and have a lovely night out. Every Friday we'd have a singsong and a few pints. He was a demon on the piano was Bill. He knew all the music hall songs. He could play 'em all." Harry dropped his voice to a conspiratorial whisper and pointed towards the grand piano, "You know what sir? Yesterday, when no one was looking, he had a go on that, just softly like. It was wonderful… and then, bless me, ten minutes later he was stone dead. 'Ere, hold up, he's on, that German bloke."

I looked across the stage and saw that Herr Johann Richter had placed himself centre stage, in front of his piano. He looked over in our direction and briskly nodded. Seeing this, Harry Small began to wind steadily on the large windlass and the heavy velvet curtains pulled gracefully apart. The audience cheered and clapped as Richter and his piano were gradually revealed. Richter bowed stiffly and once the audience was silent, he began to announce his programme for the evening, giving them a little information on each piece.

I sidled over to Holmes and whispered, "Have you observed anything of importance, Holmes?"

He shook his head and looked gravely concerned, "The assassin could be off stage somewhere or even in the audience with a silenced weapon."

I thought to lighten the conversation slightly, "You know, I consider that you were badly treated yesterday by Herr Richter. It appears that Bill Bradley was something of a pub pianist. He had a little go on Richter's piano but he didn't get caught."

Holmes wheeled round on me, his eyes ablaze, "When was this, Watson? Quickly, man!"

"Well…it was about ten minutes before he died," I stumbled.

"That's it!" cried Holmes. "It's the piano! There is a toxin on the piano keys!"

Even as he spoke, the first notes of a piano sonata could be heard. In a flash, Holmes looked around him, reached down and was to be seen running across the stage like a madman. On seeing Holmes racing towards Richter, there was a tremendous gasp from the audience. Herr Richter stopped playing and looked up just in time to have his hands and the keyboard of his beloved Bechstein doused in water from the large fire bucket wielded by Holmes.

Richter was incandescent! He made a grab for Holmes but fortunately missed. Holmes turned and ran full speed back towards me at the side of the stage with Richter in hot pursuit with his arms outstretched. This was clearly what Holmes had intended for, as Richter approached, Holmes doused him again with the contents of a second fire bucket. Seeing this debacle, Holmes was quickly seized by several stagehands but was heard to be screaming, "His hands! Wash his hands!"

Richter looked down at his hands and must have felt some slight tingling for he plunged them into a third fire bucket and began to scrub madly at them.

After a few moments, order was restored, the curtains closed and Holmes was released. I explained that I was a doctor and examined Herr Richter's hands. Apart from a little darkening at the tips, his fingers were intact. The acid and the deadly toxin had not had sufficient time to act. Holmes's quick thinking with the water had effectively flushed away any remaining chemical.

Herr Richter approached us. He stopped, stood erect and then clicked his heels together before bowing slightly. "It seems, Mr Holmes, that I owe you my life. Perhaps you are a guardian angel sent by your brother, hein?"

A rueful smile crossed Holmes's face, "Herr Richter, I am also in your debt as you inadvertently saved my life this afternoon. If you had not stopped me from playing your beautiful piano, I too would be dead."

Richter smiled and nodded but the smile faded as he asked, "Who has done this? Do you know?"

Holmes paused and then looked Richter in the eye, saying, "This act was meant to kill you in a very public manner and, by doing so, tarnish the reputation of Britain. I believe it was carried out by a criminal organisation, one that is now destined to spread throughout Europe, awakening and organising networks of criminals that I thought would not rise again. At its head is a ruthless woman, Julia Moriarty. Her name is one that you would do well to remember, Herr Richter."

Richter nodded ruefully, "I believe it is one that I will always have at my fingertips Mr Holmes." He gave a hollow laugh and began to walk away but, as he did so, he turned slightly and looking over his shoulder he called, "Say 'thank you' to your brother for me!"

Holmes turned to me, his face once more like riven stone. "My God, Watson, if he only knew. The government will no doubt make the most of this. Whitehall will bask in the glory, the Kaiser will feel indebted…and Britain has their Naval secrets… but at what cost?"

I placed my hand upon my friend's shoulder, saying, "You told the truth, Holmes. There can be no blame in that. It is for those in government to bear the guilt." I knew these words would not salve the tremendous hurt he was feeling and I could see the immense frustration of injustice raging within him. The only thing now was to return home and perhaps allow a little Laudanum to provide some retreat from the harshness of reality.

After another night of fitful sleep, I arose to find Holmes sitting in his armchair and noticed him drawing slowly on the briar pipe I had given him at the start of our first encounter with Julia Moriarty. I reached for the bell to inform Mrs Hudson that I was ready to take my breakfast, saying, "Good morning Holmes. Have you breakfasted?"

Holmes looked up, saying, "Yes, thank you Watson." Despite this assurance, I could see beside him his breakfast tray which was untouched.

It was some half an hour later that our doorbell rang and Mrs Hudson brought in a very sombre Mr John Carlisle Scott who, except for his shirt, was dressed totally in black. I pushed forwards a chair, ushering him to sit. He gave me a brief smile, sat and pulled from his jacket pocket his chequebook.

"I have come to settle my account with you Mr Holmes, I am most grateful for your kind help in the matter of finding my niece."

I felt urged to speak, "Have the police any information regarding the culprit, Mr Scott?" I asked.

Scott looked saddened. "Unfortunately not, Dr Watson. The police appear to have made little progress but have suggested it to be the work of a criminal gang."

Holmes rose from his chair and held up his hand, saying, "There is no fee Mr Scott. I did but little and I fear that I have been unable to supply any further information to the police. However, you can perhaps draw some small comfort from the fact that your niece did nothing to bring this upon herself. It appears that she inadvertently stumbled upon a plot to kill Herr Richter and, as a result, her life was forfeit. Regrettably, the identity of the person who killed your niece remains unknown."

Scott stood, his shoulders drooping in grief and despair. Reaching out his hand, he grasped Sherlock's in a solemn and sincere gesture of thanks. "I am indebted to you, Mr Holmes. My brother and his family are as grateful for your help as I am." With that, and a nod in my direction, he left our rooms.

Sitting once again, Holmes drew up his knees and remained so for several minutes, a reflective expression upon his face. "We must not close this case, Watson. At some point in the future we will snare this villain and he will most surely hang."

I sat and began to fill my pipe, turning over in my mind the events of the previous day. "Tell me, Holmes, how was the toxin applied?"

A grim expression appeared on the face of Holmes. "It was as ingenious as it was deadly, Watson. I await the confirmation of the toxicology report from Scotland Yard but it is my belief that the poison used was Curare. As you are aware, it is a black paste and when it is in contact with unbroken skin it is merely a skin irritant. It is when it enters the bloodstream that its potency as a poison begins and paralysis follows. In this instance, the Curare had been dissolved in acid, painted upon the piano keys and left to dry. The moisture from the skin of the fingers was sufficient to make this thin layer soluble again."

I was once more confused. "You say that Curare is a black paste but when I saw the piano keys yesterday there was nothing to be seen upon them."

Holmes chuckled. "Come, come, Watson, there are not only white keys on a piano keyboard. The Curare had been painted on the black keys to obscure its presence. When Bill Bradley played the piano he had been working hard and his hands were moist from his exertions. He easily picked up a little of the acid and poison. In Richter's case, he was to perform on stage before hundreds of people. Despite his arrogance, his hands could not fail to have been damp from perspiration."

I took a pull upon my pipe, saying, "Curare is not easily come by, Holmes. It is certainly not the tool of a common criminal but it is one which Julia Moriarty has knowledge of and, no doubt, has access to."

Upon saying her name, my thoughts suddenly leaped to Holmes's brother. "But what of Mycroft? Will you be able to forgive him?"

Holmes remained silent for several minutes. "At present, I am unsure…his position was extraordinarily difficult. Had he persisted in arguing against the release of Julia Moriarty, he would have been dismissed. With his departure, all semblances of intelligence and honour would also have left Whitehall. The government would have lost its finest brain. What part he played or what influence he had in the decision to 'remove' Johann Richter, I have yet to determine. It is something that I must consider at length."

This situation lasted for some weeks with no contact between the two brothers. However, during this time Holmes was in receipt of snippets of information from his own sources within Whitehall. He discovered that the Prime Minister and the Cabinet had indeed not chosen to make Mycroft Holmes privy to the details of their plans for the assassination of Johann Richter. They had feared that his fraternal ties to Sherlock and their shared hatred of Julia Moriarty might adversely affect Mycroft's judgement. With this knowledge, Holmes's renewed his contact with his brother and their relationship returned to its more usual format, that being affable indifference with a good measure of intellectual gamesmanship.

Sherlock Holmes

\-

The Severed Finger

by Dick Gillman

Table of Contents

The Severed Finger

Chapter 1 – The mystery package

It was an unseasonably foggy evening in the July of 1899 when the appearance at our door of cabby, Henry Wiggins, began the case I have here recorded as that of 'The Severed Finger'.

Holmes and I had settled down after dinner. I was engrossed in a somewhat intriguing article in 'The Lancet' on Stilton Cheese and Holmes was hidden from view by a copy of 'The Times'. The occasional plume of blue smoke rising from behind the broadsheet was the only sign that he was still awake.

The ringing of our doorbell at such a late hour was unusual and it took a minute or so for Mrs Hudson to answer the door. Of an evening, it was known to us that she busied herself with her hobby of crochet. Her latest endeavour was a rather fine tray cloth that she had proudly displayed and upon which our afternoon tea had been served. Holmes was seen to closely examine the item and Mrs Hudson beamed as Holmes complimented her upon her skills in needlecraft.

A few moments passed before her footsteps could be heard on the stairs followed by those of a much heavier person. Holmes put down his paper and looked up, listening, before going to the window and pulling aside the heavy curtain.

"Ah, I believe we are to have a visit from the uncle of young Wiggins, that is clearly his cab with 'Daisy' between the shafts and he is nowhere to be seen."

At that moment the door to our rooms opened and in walked a bespectacled and clearly miffed Mrs Hudson. Beside her stood the cabby, Henry Wiggins.

Wiggins touched his cap and then removed it saying "Evenin' Mr Holmes, Dr Watson." He stood for a moment, uncomfortably shuffling from one foot to another and glancing at Mrs Hudson. It was clear that he didn't want to say more whilst she was in the room.

Holmes nodded to Wiggins and with a grateful smile said, "Thank you Mrs Hudson, I hope our visitor didn't interrupt your crochet too much?"

Mrs Hudson's demeanour was seen to change slightly. She shook her head, "No, Mr Holmes. I had only just started a nice doily for your decanter." She turned and gave Wiggins a hard look before going back downstairs to her needlework.

Holmes ran his expert eye over Henry Wiggins and smiled. "I see that this unusually foggy weather is making you a wealthy man, Wiggins."

Henry Wiggins scratched his head, saying, "Well, there is more custom on foggy nights, Mr Holmes, folk don't want to be walking in this...but how did you know I was doing better?"

Holmes chuckled. "Well, I presume that you don't usually feed Daisy on oats when money is tight."

Wiggins's eyes grew wide. "How did you know that Mr Holmes?"

"Your boots, man. Your boots! Sticking to the side of them is some bran but also some rolled oats, a clear sign of a cabbie's prosperity."

Wiggins's face softened as he smiled, saying, "I does like to treat her when I'm a bit flush. She's a good horse and she works hard."

Holmes nodded and returned to his chair. "Now, what is it that brings you here when you should be working?"

Wiggins again shuffled. "Well, sir. It's a bit awkward. This evening I picks up this fare in Blandford Street who wants to go to Hanover Square. This bloke seems to be in a bit of a rush and asks me to hurry up a bit. He offers me an extra shilling so I goes down Marylebone Lane. It's shorter but a bit rough on the cab and the horse as they have been mending the road and that. I would normally go down James Street and onto Oxford

Street but he's impatient and pays me the fare and the extra shilling."

Holmes nodded and waved his fingers as an indication for Wiggins to continue. "Anyways, I'm feeling the damp a bit in me bones so I decides as I've got a bit extra, I'll go to the cab stand on Brook Street and have a cup of tea. There are always some other cabbies at the cafe and I can give Daisy her feed. Well, I was there about ten minutes, chatting with the lads and I goes to the front of the cab to give the lamps a bit of a wipe. I looks inside the cab to wipe the seat and there on the floor is this packet. It must have been jiggled and fallen from the fare's pocket as we drives over them new cobbles."

Wiggins paused and was now looking concerned. "I wouldn't bother you Mr Holmes but I'm worried about this." Wiggins drew from his coat a plain, white envelope with a red stain at one corner.

" I thinks it's blood...and fresh too...and what with that bit of trouble you helped me with last year...I don't wants to take it to the police myself."

Holmes sprang from his chair and took the envelope from Wiggins. Reaching for his glass, Holmes began to examine the envelope most carefully.

"Yes, I think that was a wise decision, Wiggins. It appears that the blood on the envelope has come from the contents rather than from outside."

I looked at Wiggins and on hearing this, I saw an involuntary shudder pass through his body. The colour had drained from his face and his voice stumbled, "Would …would you mind if I leaves that with you, Mr Holmes only I've left Daisy outside and…?"

Holmes looked up briefly, saying, "Yes, you had better be on your way Wiggins, I will deal with this."

Wiggins put on his cap and moved hastily towards the door but paused and looked back at Holmes. "And…and you won't…"

Holmes looked up again and waved his hand towards the door. "No, no…be on your way."

Wiggins touched his cap with his forefinger, closed the door and was off at speed down the stairs.

Holmes meanwhile had moved further towards the gaslight. "This is both intriguing and disturbing Watson. It feels from the outside to be a finger and there is more, it seems to have upon it a ring."

In truth, I almost dropped my pipe. "What? Are you sure?" I gasped.

"Yes, I fear so. The envelope is common commercial stock with no address and just two initials, 'B.M. written in black ink in a strong, cursive hand. There is a wax seal but no impressed mark. Having no address, this packet was obviously to be delivered in person."

Finding nothing more to be gleaned from the envelope, Holmes reached for his fine, Italian stiletto paper knife, a permanent memento of the Cagliari affair. I watched intently as he carefully slit the envelope. Peering inside at the contents, he moved to the dining table.

"Watson, a sheet of blotting paper and some forceps, if you will."

I scurried off to Holmes's desk and obtained a fresh sheet and laid it before him. The forceps I took from the vast array of surgical equipment that filled one whole drawer of his desk. Passing Holmes the forceps, he used them to gently remove what appeared to be a folded note. Laying this to one side for a moment, he removed from the envelope a small, slender package that appeared to be wrapped in greaseproof paper of the kind found in butchers' shops.

Holmes picked up his glass and examined the greaseproof paper before proceeding further. "This sheet has been cut from a larger one or perhaps even a roll. Two of the sides bear the distinctive 'saw-tooth' edge where the sheet has

112

been cut with a small pair of scissors with a blade of barely four inches. One side is machine cut and the other looks like it has been torn against a straight-edge."

Looking further, there could be seen a small 'pocket' of blood which had collected in one corner and it was from a pinprick in this that the blood had leaked through to the envelope.

Holmes began to carefully open the greaseproof paper and the object within was then revealed. I moved forwards, eager to more clearly see the contents. There, before us, was what appeared to be a man's severed ring finger with a gold signet ring still in place.

I could not stop myself from exclaiming, "Good Lord, Holmes! This is macabre!"

Holmes placed the opened greaseproof paper packet and the finger onto the sheet of blotting paper. Taking up his glass, Holmes examined the finger minutely. When he had finished, he stood for a moment, his right forefinger held vertically against his lips before saying, "As a medical man, I would value your opinion of this, Watson.

I moved even closer and took the liberty of using Holmes's glass to examine the finger. "It is clearly no medical student's dissecting room prank, Holmes. The finger appears to be quite fresh and likely to have been recently removed from a living human being. It has been severed professionally at the third joint and I can see no disease… but why leave the ring on the finger?"

Holmes took up his glass and with meticulous care, lifted the finger in his forceps. "Looking at the skin texture, this is the finger from a young man of probably less than thirty years of age. He is, I would say, from the leisured classes, fastidious about his appearance as his fingernail is, for the most part, exquisitely manicured. However, there is dirt beneath the nail and it is slightly torn at one side. The dirt is, I believe, from an environment quite out of character for its owner and the tear implies that there has perhaps been a struggle."

Then, using a clean handkerchief, he slipped off the gold signet ring. This he closely examined, both the engraving on the face of the ring and the impressed marks on the interior.

Chapter 2 – A cryptic note

Seeming to be satisfied, Holmes now turned his attention to the note. With immeasurable care, he opened it and read the message written upon it.

"Listen to this, Watson, 'Unfortunately you have chosen to ignore me. Before you is the tragic consequence of your inaction. The delivery to the Reichstag must be made at noon on the 17th. Final instructions will be given when we meet. Reserve a table by the window at Lyon's Tea Shop in Piccadilly for exactly 1:30 pm on Wednesday the 15th. Be alone and in plain view'."

Holmes looked thoughtful; he stood in silence for several minutes before putting down his glass and walking to the bookcase. Selecting his copy of de Brett's, he flipped through it, pausing briefly before returning it to its shelf. A quizzical look was now on Holmes's face as he retired to his chair. Reaching for his pipe, he lit it and sat in silence, drawing occasionally upon it.

After several minutes my inquisitive nature could not be denied. "Holmes! We find a human finger that has been dropped in a London cab together with a vile message and you have nothing to say?"

Holmes blew out a steady stream of blue smoke. "All in good time, Watson. Pray allow me a moment to consider the facts." With that, Holmes drew up his knees and entered that inner state where almost all external stimuli were excluded.

I knew that it was impossible to rush Holmes. He needed the time to consider the questions that had been raised by his observations and to evaluate all the possible outcomes.

It was some ten minutes before Holmes once more became animated.

Turning to me, Holmes asked, "Tell me Watson, what would you suppose might be the reason to send someone a severed finger?"

I thought for a moment. "Well, I find it difficult to imagine a reason but the only thing I can think of for such harm is, perhaps, revenge…but it is a most violent act for simply ignoring someone."

Holmes again looked thoughtful. "Yes, revenge is a possibility, although I think in this case, the motive is not that of revenge. I am of the opinion that someone has been kidnapped and is being held against their will. The reason for the dismemberment may then be one of blackmail."

I jumped in my chair, crying "Blackmail? You cannot seriously be saying that this dismemberment is part of some dreadful blackmail plot?"

Holmes's face was like stone. "I am very much afraid that it is… and one that I fear has already been dismissed as a hoax." He looked at me coldly and then began to tell me his interpretation of the evening's grim events.

Sitting back with his pipe, Holmes began. "The package was intended for someone with the initials B.M. This is most likely to be the head of the household, someone with influence as the writer expects the recipient to be able to fulfil his demands. It was seemingly to be delivered in person to an address in Hanover Square. Now Watson, who might this person be? Obviously, someone of considerable wealth to have such an address. Does a person of considerable wealth and power with the initials B.M. spring to mind?"

I thought for a moment and then shook my head, "I fear I am at a loss here, Holmes."

Holmes smiled grimly. He continued, "I am somewhat at an advantage, Watson for I have closely examined the signet ring and referred to de Brett's. I recognised some elements of the crest engraved upon it. Unfortunately, I am unable to positively identify the family and will need to enquire of Sir Basil Brookfield, a Herald at the College of Arms in Queen Victoria Street." With that he reached for his notebook and dashed off a telegram before ringing the bell.

Chapter 3 – Seeking the help of a Herald

The following morning Holmes was keen to proceed and shortly after nine a.m. we were travelling at a good pace towards the College of Arms. Holmes was bright-eyed and leaned towards me, eager to talk above the noise of the city and the rumble of the cab.

"Have you ever met Sir Basil Brookfield, Watson?" asked Holmes with a strange twinkle in his eye.

I thought for a moment, "Err…no, I don't believe I have."

At this, Holmes slapped his knee and cried "Ha!" He then he sat back in the cab with a smile that would have befitted a Cheshire cat and would not be drawn to say more.

The cab stopped in Carter Street and it was with some trepidation that I descended from the cab, unsure as to what I might find on meeting the Herald. We walked the short distance to the College; a strangely unbalanced, 'U' shaped building that faced New Queen Victoria Street.

On entering the central courtyard, a short flight of steps brought us to the porch which provided shelter for the front door. Holmes rang the bell and we waited but a few moments before a liveried servant appeared. Holmes's telegram had made the college aware of our intended visit and we were swiftly ushered through various vestibules and corridors, each heavily decorated with the trappings of heraldry. Finally, our guide stopped outside a very handsomely carved mahogany door and tapped gently upon it. I noticed that the servant had retreated several steps from the door and a look of concern was upon his face.

Suddenly, the door was flung open and a wild-eyed and dishevelled figure stood before us. His grey hair was un-brushed and sprouted from his head at somewhat improbable angles. My first impression was that his rather pinched face resembled that of a startled gnome. His jacket was ill fitting, worn and patched at the elbows. This was put to shame by a fine, though incongruous lavender-coloured waistcoat. The trousers matched the jacket for wear and the shoes had a tired and unpolished look to them.

"Yes?" enquired the man in a thin but powerful voice. Its owner's eyes flashed from Holmes to me and then back to Holmes in a manner I had seen in patients who were used to having frequent visits by the bailiffs.

Holmes smiled. "Sir Basil, how nice to meet you again. I'm Sherlock Holmes and this is my friend and colleague, Dr Watson. You have had my telegram, I take it?"

Sir Basil Brookfield looked again at us and then waved dismissively at the servant. "Yes, I've had it…Holmes, you say…ah, yes, I recall your last visit, you wanted information regarding the paternity of the Duke of…"

Holmes cut short any further indiscretion by gently ushering Sir Basil back into his office saying, "Quite, shall we go inside?"

Sir Basil walked back into his office and then spun on his heel. "Watson, you say? Do you have relatives in Trowbridge?"

I was a little taken aback and stammered, "Well, no, but I did have an aunt in Devizes…"

"Pity, yes…yes…Hmmm…pity" was all the response I received from this strange gentleman.

I looked to Holmes who was trying most earnestly not to chuckle. Holmes gathered himself together and produced the signet ring from his pocket. "This is the signet ring, Sir Basil. I would be most grateful if you could identify the family crest for us."

Sir Basil took the ring and reached into his jacket pocket. From it he withdrew a tiny pair of spectacles which had one of the lenses held in place merely by a smear of sealing wax. Perching these on the very tip of his nose, he skipped across the office towards one of the large leaded windows of the College. From his other jacket pocket he pulled out a magnifying glass with a handle made from what appeared to be the tip of a stags antler.

120

As if reading my mind, Sir Basil remarked, "Ah, a gift from a grateful Scottish Earl…mmm…so what have we here? Yes, Per Pall, a lion's head erased, 3 bezants and a hind's head…hmmm." Sir Basil again skipped his way towards a large mahogany bookcase and from it removed a mighty, leather-bound tome. After some moments of flicking through the pages he paused. "Martindale! Yes, Martindale." Smiling, he held out the ring towards Holmes who took it gratefully.

I glanced at Holmes and saw a look of satisfaction upon his face. This had obviously confirmed Holmes's own suspicions regarding the provenance of the ring.

Holmes smiled saying, "Thank you, Sir Basil, you have been most helpful."

Brookfield blinked, briefly cocked his head to one side and muttered a farewell. Taking that as a dismissal, we left the way we had come and within half an hour we were back in our rooms.

Once settled, Holmes removed the signet ring from his pocket, sat back and was seen to be turning it over and over in his fingers with his eyes closed. I was intrigued as to what Holmes's thoughts were on first sight of the ring.

"Did you suspect that the ring belonged to the Martindales?" I asked.

Holmes opened his eyes and looked once more at the ring. "Yes, my brief glance at de Brett's suggested it...but I could not be sure. The crest certainly contained elements that pointed to the ring belonging to a member of the Martindale family. My examination of it also established that it was not a modern piece. The hallmark bears witness to it having been made some several decades ago."

I rubbed my chin and tried to search my memory for the name, saying, "Hmmm, Martindale...Martindale. The only person of that name that I recall was an officer from my army days, Brigadier Sir Brian Martindale. He retired and became the chairman of the Maxim Nordenfelt Gun and Ammunition Company."

A grim look was now upon Holmes's face as he continued, "Precisely, Watson, the initials on the envelope indicate that the recipient was to be Sir Brian Martindale. Bearing no name, it also suggests that the package was to be conveyed to him personally."

I nodded slowly as I considered Holmes's deduction.

Holmes rose and made his way to the bookcase and once more took up his copy of de Brett's. "Now, only a very close family member would be allowed to wear the ring, so to whom might the finger belong?" He flicked through the pages until he found the entry he wanted. "Ah, yes.

Looking at the Martindale line, Sir Brian has but one son, Edward Martindale. I believe the finger to belong to him."

The full impact of this was now upon me, questions were now whirling in my head. "You said blackmail, Holmes, but the note in the envelope made no threat...and why not just send the ring?"

Holmes's face became even sterner. "I believe that this communication with its grim enclosure had been sent because of a lack of response to a previous demand. Its purpose is two fold. It is to prove the identity of the captive and it is also a brutal display of intent to cause further harm should the kidnappers' demands not be met. This is a grave instrument of fear designed to intimidate Sir Brian."

Holmes stood and began to pace, a forefinger placed against his lips. "Given Sir Brian's position, I must inform Mycroft for this may entail a threat to the security of our nation. Furthermore, it is the government who has let lose this hound from hell, the one who is responsible for this act."

It took me but a moment to understand what Holmes was saying..."Moriarty!"

Holmes nodded, saying, "This intrigue, this total lack of humanity is her trademark. She must be stopped and Edward Martindale found before any further harm befalls him."

I was gravely concerned by Holmes's analysis. "Do you believe that Edward Martindale is still alive?"

Holmes stopped pacing and stood before me. "Yes, I believe so. It is in her interest to keep him alive. You observed how cleanly the finger had been removed? It was done with a purpose and by someone with surgical knowledge and skill. Edward Martindale must be kept alive in case they need to make another show of intent."

I was appalled at the thought of a surgeon becoming involved in such an act. Indeed, I shuddered at the thought of further fingers or even limbs being removed and used to convince the Martindale family of the determination of Edward's captors.

Without further ado, Holmes reached for his notebook and dashed off a telegram to summon Mycroft to our rooms at10 a.m. the following morning.

Chapter 4 – A meeting with Mycroft

The next day we breakfasted early and whilst waiting for Mycroft, I continued with my perusal of 'The Lancet'. Holmes, however, was to be seen scanning 'The Times'.

Precisely at 10 a.m. a Hansom could be heard pulling up outside our front door. A few moments later this was followed by the familiar tread of Mycroft upon our stairs. He no longer bothered to ring the doorbell and the briefest twitch of the net curtains showed that Mrs Hudson on the floor below had seen and approved of our visitor.

Moments later, Mycroft swept into our rooms. With a brief nod to me, he removed his hat and coat and sat, waiting expectantly for Holmes to appear from behind his copy of 'The Times'.

A disembodied voice from behind the newspaper asked, "Watson, be a good fellow and ring for Mrs Hudson. She has the item that I wish to show Mycroft."

Of course, I knew to what he was referring and I duly rang the bell. After two or three minutes Mrs Hudson appeared carrying a small package. Holmes folded his newspaper and looked towards his brother as the package was offered to him. Mrs Hudson was still in our rooms and standing beside Mycroft when he opened the greaseproof paper. Once the contents were revealed, she was seen to leap three steps back and to cling to the doorframe. Her hand went to her mouth and it was a few moments before she was able to say anything.

"Oh my word, Mr Holmes. I kept that thing cool as you asked...it was in the icebox with the mutton chops!" With that, she fled from the room and was to be heard racing down the stairs.

Mycroft appeared totally unimpressed, saying, "I take a very dim view of being summoned half way across London in order to witness my brother playing a practical joke on his housekeeper."

Mycroft rose and was about to collect his hat and coat when Holmes's voice stopped him in his tracks. "I believe this to be the work of a certain Julia Moriarty and it is designed to frighten and intimidate Sir Brian Martindale. I also believe that this is the ring finger of Edward Martindale, the son of Sir Brian. It is, I fear, an attempt to extort some benefit from him as the Chairman of the Maxim Nordenfelt Gun and Ammunition Company."

Mycroft turned towards his brother. I could see that much of the colour had drained from Mycroft's face and he returned to sit facing Sherlock. "Tell me all that you know Sherlock for this is a matter of national importance."

For the next few minutes, Sherlock recounted all that had occurred and presented his deductions to his brother. I looked towards Mycroft who now looked even paler. It was clear that he was privy to information that we were not.

Holmes stood and pulled from his waistcoat pocket the note that had accompanied the dismembered finger and passed it to Mycroft. "This was inside the envelope with the finger. What do you infer from the reference to the Reichstag, Mycroft? I know how relations with the Germans are somewhat delicate at present and also the importance of the Reichstag as an edifice in Germany…but I feel that this is not the meaning here."

Holmes paused for a moment as he once again asked himself questions and considered possibilities within that great mind of his. It was as though he was verbalising his own thoughts.

With his forefinger once again raised to his lips, he pondered, "Given the current level of unrest in the British Empire, especially on the African continent and the demand for modern weaponry..." Holmes's body suddenly stiffened and became rigid. "No! Of course! It is not a location, it is a vessel!"

Holmes leapt forwards and rummaged madly amongst the pile of newspapers beside his chair. "Ah, yes! The 'Reichstag' is due to sail on the 17th, in three days time, destined for Lourenco Marques."

Mycroft looked distinctly uncomfortable. "I will be totally frank with you, Sherlock. Her

Majesty's Government is greatly concerned regarding the acquisition of weapons by the Boers. The public were grievously led to believe that the Boers had been secretly arming themselves for many years by smuggling arms in shipments of furniture and other innocent goods. Unfortunately, this is not the case. It is a misconception that the government has been keen to encourage both in the press and, I'm ashamed to say, within parliament."

I was shocked! Surely Her Majesty's Government would not deceive the nation or, indeed, parliament so?

Mycroft continued, "The fact is that in the last 18 months, British and European companies have openly supplied huge amounts of arms and ammunition to the Boers. Much of the ordinance being shipped in German flagged vessels. Only now is the government trying to curtail this practice. Exports of weapons and ammunition overseas are to be heavily restricted or even prohibited."

I looked towards Mycroft and saw that he was very troubled.

"This is indeed most serious Sherlock, I am grateful that you have brought it to my attention. I must visit Sir Brian and make enquiries regarding his son and to examine any previous communications he may have received from Julia Moriarty."

Holmes turned and began to approach his brother at this point. "I intend to involve myself fully in this, Mycroft, as we both have a vested interest in a successful outcome...although these interests may prove to be quite different. I will continue in this case for the good of the nation and for the safe return of Edward Martindale. In order to do this I must act, initially at least, alone."

Again I was shocked. Alone? What was to be my role in all of this?

Holmes continued, his voice growing in strength, "However, you are in my debt, Mycroft, and as such I require you to take Watson with you when you visit Sir Brian."

Mycroft stood and fumed. "Quite impossible! This is a matter of national security, I could not possibly..."

"Mycroft!" Holmes's voice boomed across our drawing room. "This is not a request, it is a prerequisite for my continued assistance in this matter. Look upon this as some small atonement by the government for the untold damage caused by Moriarty's release."

With supressed anger plainly visible within Mycroft, he gave his brother the briefest of nods to indicate his acceptance of Holmes's condition. Holmes handed Edward Martindale's ring to Mycroft and seemingly within moments, Mycroft and I were on our way down the stairs and summoning a Hansom.

Chapter 5 – Sir Brian Martindale

We travelled in silence as we sped towards
Hanover Square and the residence of Sir Brian
Martindale. In truth, I had not the slightest idea what
Holmes intended to do whilst I was with Mycroft
but no doubt he would recount it all to me that
evening over dinner.

As we approached Hanover Square, it
became apparent that Mycroft already knew the
residence of Sir Brian as he directed the cabby
towards a large Georgian townhouse of considerable
proportions. The building was double-fronted, on
three stories and painted white to match the others in
the row. The front garden was lawned and well
tended. I observed that the whole property was
surrounded by high, black painted and spiked, cast
iron railings.

At the front door Mycroft turned to me,
saying "I would be grateful, Watson, if you would
leave the talking to me and only observe."

I nodded in acceptance as I was unsure as to
what role Sherlock had intended for me. Mycroft
lifted the large, ornate lions head doorknocker and
rapped loudly upon it.

After but a few moments a liveried servant
opened the door and was seemingly about to ask us
our business when a voice behind him called out
"Mycroft! Good Lord, what are you doing here?"

The servant bowed and discreetly left. Mycroft and I found ourselves looking into the hallway of the house as a gentleman approached us with his hand outstretched in welcome.

Mycroft moved forward and into the hallway with his hand outstretched and grasped that of Sir Brian. "Good morning Brian, I am here on a rather delicate matter and would like to speak to you in private."

Sir Brian nodded and then glanced in my direction before returning his attention to Mycroft and raising his eyebrows very slightly.

Mycroft, ever astute, saw the gesture and responded "Ah, yes. This is a colleague of my brother Sherlock who is assisting me in this matter. Is there somewhere where we might..?"

Sir Brian turned and led us deeper into the house and into a room that at first I took to be the family library. The room itself had a grand Georgian fireplace to one side and windows on the opposite side that gave a splendid view of Hanover Square. The end walls were, for the most part, lined with mahogany bookcases filled with leather-bound volumes. These, together with mementos from his army career identified this to be more of a gentleman's study.

Sir Brian moved to sit behind his desk and motioned for us to pull up two chairs to face him.

Smiling, Sir Brian said, "Gentlemen, you have my full attention."

Mycroft shuffled awkwardly and then leant forward, saying rather formally, "Sir Brian, when did you last see your son?"

Sir Brian's demeanour changed slightly. He recognised the formality of Mycroft's question and became more serious. Locking eyes now with Mycroft, he replied, "Well, let me see…he came here for a little supper just over a week ago. Why do you ask?"

Again Mycroft shuffled in his chair. "You know that by way of my position in Whitehall, I have contacts who, on occasions, bring me intelligence. A letter and your son's signet ring have been intercepted on their way to you. After reading the letter, I believe your son to be in some considerable danger."

Mycroft reached into his jacket pocket and placed Edward's signet ring on the leather surface of Sir Brian's desk.

Reaching forwards, Sir Brian picked up the ring and it was clear from his expression that he recognised it immediately. "It was my grandfather's, I gave it to Edward on his twenty-first birthday. How was it obtained?"

Mycroft's voice softened slightly. "Brian, you must be totally open with me, your son's life may depend on it. Have you had any communications that indicate that your son may have lost his liberty?"

I could see Sir Brian blink as Mycroft's question hit home. "How could you know? I thought it a hoax! I received a letter, delivered by hand, from some lunatic wanting me to give him six Maxim machine guns in exchange for Edward. Lunacy! Pure and simple, Mycroft!"

Mycroft appeared to be momentarily stunned by what had been demanded. Gathering himself together, he edged forward in his seat. His demeanour was now that of a gun dog with the scent of the quarry in its nostrils.

"I fear that the letter was in earnest and I hope to heaven you have kept it for it is an important link to those who hold your son."

The colour was now seen to have drained from Sir Brian's face. He pushed back his chair and opened the top drawer of his fine, walnut desk. From it he withdrew an envelope upon which I could see had been written the initials B.M.

Sir Brian looked suddenly fatigued. "I had a mind to simply throw it in the grate but then thought I might pass it on to our local constabulary."

Reaching forwards, Mycroft took the envelope from Sir Brian, opened it and read the contents before passing it to me. I took it eagerly and read the following…

"Sir Brian, your son is currently our guest. He has come to no harm at present but his welfare cannot be guaranteed unless our demands are met. In order to obtain his release without harm, you are to arrange the supply of six Maxim machine guns in full working order. They are to be readied within the week for shipment on the vessel 'Reichstag' which is currently docked at Tilbury. Failure to agree to these terms will have severe and permanent consequences for your son.

Your house is being watched and to signal your acceptance of these terms, you must place a ribbon around the knocker on your front door'.

Seeing that I had read the note, Mycroft took it from me and slipped it into his coat pocket. "I presume that as you thought this to be a hoax, you did not follow the instructions?"

Sir Brian was incensed. "Certainly not! I thought it total rot!"

Mycroft slowly shook his head. "I fear it was not. The second message, which was intercepted, gave further instructions for you to ready the guns for delivery. It also provided proof of their intent to harm your son should you not comply."

Sir Brian, a fine soldier, now found himself in an impossible position. As we watched, his hands went to his head and he covered his face. "What am I to do Mycroft?"

Mycroft replied in a calm voice, saying, "My brother has some experience in these matters. My counsel would be to place your trust in him and allow him to act on your behalf."

Removing his hands, Sir Brian looked directly at Mycroft. "He can help? Truly?"

Mycroft nodded and extended his hand across the desk to Sir Brian who shook it most gratefully.

After somewhat solemn goodbyes, Mycroft and I went our separate ways with the understanding that any further developments were to be sent by telegram to the other party.

Chapter 6 – Pork chops and paper

I hailed a Hansom and returned to Baker Street. Finding that Holmes was still absent, I settled down again in my armchair with my copy of 'The Lancet'. I must have dozed off as the next thing that I recall was Holmes bounding into the room, looking very pleased with himself and carrying what looked like a very thin roll of wallpaper.

Clearing any papers that were on our dining table with one sweep of his arm, Holmes proceeded to unroll the paper he had been carrying. He secured the paper at each corner with a few books, which he snatched from our bookcase.

"Holmes!" I cried, "What the devil are you doing?"

Holmes held up his hand with his palm towards me in order to silence me. Immediately, he took out his glass and began to minutely examine the cut edge of the roll of paper. Once satisfied, he then carefully compared the paper to that in which the severed finger had been wrapped.

With a large smile, Holmes turned to me and announced, "They match! We have them, Watson! We have them!"

I was now fully awake and gasped, "What? You have found Edward Martindale?"

Holmes flung himself into his chair and reached for his pipe, saying, "Not quite, but I know their bolthole; a house in George Street, a few doors from St James's church."

I dropped my copy of 'The Lancet' and urged Holmes to tell me more.

Settling into his chair, Holmes filled his pipe whilst he recounted how he had spent the morning.

"My first port of call was the 'Lyon's Tea Shop' in Piccadilly. She has chosen this particular venue for a purpose, Watson, and on visiting the establishment, the reason became clear. The front window has a commanding view over Piccadilly and it would be impossible for anyone to approach the premises with any degree of stealth. I also observed that there are exits leading to a maze of back alleys, which would need a veritable army to secure. Yes, she has chosen the venue for the meeting well."

Holmes lit his pipe and drew upon it before continuing, "I made the reservation for the table and then left for my second destination. Hailing a Hansom, I directed the cabby to Blandford Street. You will recall that that was the place where Henry Wiggins picked up his fare and I had a mind to, perhaps, do a little shopping for some pork chops."

I was stunned! Here was Holmes attempting to locate the hiding place of a vicious, condemned killer and was being distracted by the thought of buying pork chops!

"Good Lord, Holmes! What possessed you?" I spluttered.

Holmes smiled and wagged his finger at me in mock reproach. "Fear not Watson, it was not the chops that were of interest…it was their wrappings!"

Of course! I remembered that the severed finger had been wrapped in greaseproof paper of the kind commonly found in Butchers' shops.

Holmes continued his discourse. "There are, I found, three butchers' shops in the vicinity of Blandford Street and I visited each in turn. Two of them had pre-cut squares of greaseproof paper used for wrapping the raw meat whilst the third I found most intriguing! On entering the shop I noticed that beside the wooden butcher's block there was a cast iron stand rather like that of a small mangle but with a single, continuous roll of greaseproof paper mounted upon it. On further inspection, I noticed that a heavy metal blade rested along the length of the paper. As I observed the butcher serving the customer in front of me, I saw him draw off a length of paper. Then, with an upward movement, he tore off the piece against the straight-edge before using it to wrap the meat."

"Just like the piece around the finger!" I exclaimed.

"Precisely Watson and my examination of it proves it. The minute indentations in the blade of the straight edge transfer to the hard greaseproof paper and are like a fingerprint."

Eager to learn more, I asked, "Did you engage the butcher in conversation?"

Holmes smiled and nodded. "Yes, he was a most obliging and garrulous fellow. I told him that I had an interest in brass rubbing and had been to the nearby church of St. James but had forgotten my roll of rubbing paper."

"Bravo! Go on, go on!" cried I, eager for Holmes to continue.

Holmes blew out a thin stream of smoke before saying, "The butcher kindly offered to sell me a yard of greaseproof paper for tuppence which I promptly bought. As if in passing, I asked him if any other customers bought paper from the roll."

I was now on the edge of my seat, "Yes, yes…"

Holmes had a wicked smile upon his face. "He replied that it was really most unusual…but only the previous week one of his regular customers, a Mr Charles Grey, who lives round the corner in

George Street, had asked for a foot length to wrap a brace of pigeon."

I sat for several minutes turning over in my mind what Holmes had said and I was concerned that the evidence was incomplete.

"Holmes, forgive me but I am unsure as to how you can be so certain that you have found their lair. The greaseproof paper around the finger may match that which you obtained today but this Charles Grey fellow may well have bought the paper for the purpose that he told the butcher."

"Ha!" cried Holmes. "I will make a detective of you yet, Watson! You are quite correct, I needed to find this Grey fellow's lodging and observe who came and went. It took very little effort; a sixpence to a grocer's delivery boy was sufficient for the task. After a brief reconnoitre of the area, I found that the lounge bar of the public house at the corner of George Street gave me an excellent view of the Grey residence. After an hour, my patience was rewarded."

Holmes rose from his armchair and was then to be seen rummaging through our newspaper scrapbook for the year 1894.

Gathering up the volume, he carried it over to me. Placing it in my lap, he pointed to a yellowing newspaper clipping which bore a photograph of a middle aged, bespectacled man in a pin-striped suit.

In a triumphant voice, Holmes cried, "That is the fellow that I saw arriving at the property, Watson!"

I looked at the clipping and gasped. Before me was a photograph of a man despised by the medical profession, a surgeon who had been struck off for gross misconduct. He had been sentenced to five years in prison after carrying out illegal surgical procedures on wealthy unmarried ladies who found themselves in an unfortunate condition.

Chapter 7 – Tea with Julia Moriarty

I still could not believe it. "You saw Fritz Hofmann? Are you sure Holmes? I thought he had returned to Vienna after his release."

Holmes shook his head. "It was Hofmann, smartly dressed as always and I noted that he was carrying a black, leather Gladstone, no doubt to carry the tools of his profession."

The enormity of what Holmes had just said suddenly engulfed me. "You…you mean that you think he is the one that…"

Holmes's face was like granite. "Indeed I do. Who better to remove a finger than a disgraced surgeon who will do anything if the reward is high enough? I would imagine that the Boers are paying Julia Moriarty handsomely for the Maxims."

Gathering my composure, I managed to ask, "Do you then believe that Edward Martindale is confined at the property and if so, could he not be freed?"

Holmes began to pace, a clear sign that he was unsettled. "I believe he is there but an attempt to free him from that house would be futile. I went to the rear of the property and it leads into several alleyways. The rear windows are all heavily barred and by the time entry had been made, Edward Martindale would most certainly be dead. We must remember, Watson, that the people who hold him have already committed crimes that would send them to the gallows. They are fearless brutes who have nothing to lose."

I felt at a loss. "What is to be done then, Holmes?"

Holmes stopped pacing. It was as though the mists had cleared and clarity had returned. "I must be the one who meets with Moriarty. Sir Brian cannot for I fear for what he might do when faced with his son's captor. The consequences for his family would be unthinkable."

Rising from my chair I said in as firm a voice as I could muster, "Then I shall come too. I know what she is capable of and my service revolver has never failed me."

Holmes looked across at me and smiled, saying, "Thank you Watson, ever reliable."

We spent Wednesday morning nurturing our own thoughts and after a light luncheon eaten almost in silence, the afternoon saw us making our way to Piccadilly. On arrival at the tea-room I noticed that the clientele was quite varied. There were couples, single gentlemen and single ladies. Indeed, it was one of the few places in London thought to be respectable for single young ladies to meet friends. In the front window was a table with two chairs facing each other. Upon the table was a small double-sided card that announced that the table was 'Reserved'. Holmes sat at one side of this table whilst I moved to sit one table away, a little further back into the room in a position where I could follow proceedings with, I thought, some anonymity. At 1:35pm a gentleman carrying a folded newspaper entered the tea-room and after looking around, came and sat opposite me at my table. The waitress came and took our orders and as I looked up, I saw an auburn haired young woman enter the tea-room and sit at the table occupied by Holmes. I stiffened involuntarily and felt some comfort from the weight of my service revolver in my jacket pocket.

It was at that moment that the gentleman opposite me spoke. "I would be grateful if you were to put both your hands on the table, Dr Watson."

I was taken aback and looked more closely at the fellow. Only then did I see the muzzle of his Mauser, with the familiar box magazine, pointing directly at my heart from inside the folded newspaper.

"Please, Dr Watson. If you look around the room you will see that there are four other gentlemen with folded newspapers on their table. We don't want any senseless loss of life."

I looked around and saw the truth in what he said. I had not noticed before but at four other tables, each one with a clear field of fire, there sat a man with a folded newspaper on the table with his hand resting casually upon it. As I placed my hands on the table I felt completely impotent. I could not protect Holmes and any attempt to detain Julia Moriarty would have resulted in pointless slaughter.

In truth, she did not seem at all bemused to see Holmes and from my position a bare three feet away, I was able to follow their conversation.

Pulling in her chair, she said, "Ah, Mr Holmes. Why am I not surprised to see you?"

Holmes's face was rigid. "I assume, madam, it is because you would perhaps suspect that a severed finger found in a Hansom by a cabby who plies his trade close to Baker Street would bring it directly to me."

Julia Moriarty smiled, saying, "Ah, so that is where it was found. I feared that I would have to repeat the communication enclosing, perhaps, an ear. Something that the family would recognise… the all important signet ring having been lost."

Holmes stiffened. For a dreadful moment I thought that he would spring across the table and squeeze the life from her. I made a slight movement to rise but the steely muzzle of the Mauser opposite me nudged upwards an inch or so, just to remind me of its presence and to keep me in my place.

Moriarty continued, "I take it that your presence indicates that Sir Brian is willing to accept his side of the bargain?"

146

Showing immense control, Holmes could only nod.

She smiled again… but a chill now entered her voice. "The crates containing the items are to be brought in a wagon to the dockside and laid out in two rows of three so that they may be easily opened and the contents inspected. There will be no escort for the wagon. If any police or troops are seen in the area of the dock, then Edward Martindale will surely perish. Similarly, if I do not return within an hour of my departure, he will perish."

Julia Moriarty sat back and mockingly rebuked Holmes. "I do believe that you are even less talkative than the last time we sat together."

Holmes's voice was like ice, "I have very little to say to a woman who can disfigure an innocent young man in order to blackmail his father. What proof have I that Edward Martindale is still alive?"

Again she smiled. Turning her head to look out of the window, she slightly raised her hand. Holmes and I both turned to follow her gaze and as we did so, a closed carriage, which had been waiting some fifty yards away, set off from the kerb. As it passed the tea-room, the face of a young man, his left arm pinioned to display a bandaged hand, could be seen in the window of the carriage.

Holmes moved to stand but the glint of nickel in Julia Moriarty's hand made him pause. "We will meet again on the 17th, Mr Holmes."

With that she rose and left. The fellow opposite me touched his hat and almost as one, the five men in the tearoom rose and followed her out of the door and towards a waiting carriage.

I moved to Holmes's side. He was rigid, beside himself with anger. "That woman, Watson! That woman! She is the very embodiment of evil. When she is caught, I swear that I shall be the one who places the noose around her neck. She will not cheat death a second time."

Chapter 8 – The 'Reichstag'

I imagine that we both spent a somewhat sleepless night following our meeting with Julia Moriarty. I myself could not clear my mind of that dreadful image of Edward Martindale with his bandaged hand at the window of the carriage.

The 16th dawned and was a hive of activity. Holmes disappeared for much of the day arranging the transport of the guns. He also had several meetings with Mycroft, the details of which I was not privy to. By late afternoon it seemed that all was in place. Holmes returned, drained from his exertions. The poor fellow barely had the energy to have a bite of supper before retiring.

The 17th was much calmer. We breakfasted and I made sure that my service revolver was cleaned and loaded. Holmes appeared more relaxed than the previous day. I however, was like a coiled spring.

"Are you not going to arm yourself, Holmes?" I asked.

Holmes shook his head, saying calmly, "I feel that it will not be necessary." I looked rather quizzically at him but he would say no more.

Hailing a cab, we headed off towards our rendezvous with the wagon and the German vessel, 'Reichstag'. We said very little on our journey and soon we were at Tilbury docks. The port was full of merchantmen both large and small. Some were the coastal luggers that plied their trade between the ports of Great Britain. Others were mighty carriers of cargo from faraway lands. I watched, fascinated, as the dockside cranes loaded and unloaded cargo onto the dockside. As we waited, small ferries came and went, their shrill whistles announcing their departure or arrival at the quayside.

I looked at my pocket-watch as the wagon, drawn by two fine bay horses, pulled up on the dock alongside the waiting ship. It was exactly twelve o'clock, the time specified in the note. Looking towards the ship, I observed that the flag on the stern fluttered gently in the breeze, revealing then hiding the name of the vessel, "Reichstag", and the name of its home port of Hamburg.

I realised now that the choice of vessel to carry this cargo was not random. Choosing to send the weapons in a German flagged vessel would ensure their safe passage. The British Government would not dare to intercept and board a German vessel in international waters.

The horses of the wagon stood in their traces and snorted. Tiny sparks flared as they stamped their iron-clad hooves impatiently on the stone flagged dock.

Holmes touched my sleeve and inclined his head slightly in the direction from where two closed carriages were approaching along the dock. "If I am not mistaken, this is she and her entourage."

Looking towards the carriages, I saw that the first had stopped some fifty yards away and from it had spilled six men whom I thought were unseasonably dressed in long coats.

I pointed discreetly towards the men saying, "Do these fellows appear to be a little overdressed, Holmes?"

Holmes nodded. "Yes, but what better way to conceal a long weapon?"

The men fanned out from the carriage and took up watchful positions on the dock. I could see that they were ever alert. Their heads were constantly moving as they scanned the surrounding buildings, the approach to the dock and even the structure of the vessel itself. As if to confirm Holmes's suspicion, the open coat of one of the men was lifted slightly by the breeze and I caught a glimpse of a Mauser C96 pistol with its wooden stock attached.

The second carriage had now drawn near and I could see that across the knees of the fellow beside the driver was a similarly wooden-stocked Mauser pistol. The carriage slowed to a stop and the door opened. Two muscular, hard faced men stepped out followed by a slender, female figure dressed in a fashionable outfit that would not have been out of place on Oxford Street. The men flanked her as she approached, their hands concealed within their coats.

"Ah, Mr Holmes. I trust that Sir Brian has kept his side of the bargain and has not been so foolish as to try and deceive me, filling the crates with scrap iron or has, so to speak, spiked the guns?"

Holmes's expression was like granite and he spoke with a tone that matched it. "No, he is true to his word, the six crates are arranged for easy inspection and contain the items you demanded."

Julia Moriarty's face showed a thin smile. "I know you to be an honest man, Mr Holmes, but I am certain that your brother and Her Majesty's Government would prefer that these weapons were not exported."

She raised the gloved forefinger of her right hand slightly and one of the men flanking her barked out a command. From her carriage, a small, thin man appeared carrying a crowbar. Looking about him, he scurried to the wagon and climbed aboard. Opening each of the six cases in turn, he expertly checking the firing mechanism and then the barrel of each of the six Maxim machine guns. Seeming satisfied, he closed each of the wooden crates and nodded towards Julia Moriarty before once more scurrying back to the carriage.

Julia Moriarty smiled a little more broadly. "It would appear that we have a deal, Mr Holmes. We will keep our side of the bargain once the 'Reichstag' has left British territorial waters, which will, I believe, be in approximately three hours time."

Holmes simply nodded; he seemed unable to respond and simply raised his arm as a signal for the nearest dockside crane to lower its hook that was already festooned with loops of chain. Moriarty's two bodyguards climbed into the wagon and stacked the six cases as two columns of three, slipping the chains beneath them. At their signal, the crane billowed a great cloud of steam as its engine took up the slack and began to raise the cases towards the deck of the waiting vessel.

I felt anger building within me. For some considerable time I had held my tongue in this matter but now I was not to be denied.

In something of a stage whisper I said, "This cannot be, Holmes! One man's life cannot outweigh those of the hundreds of British troops who may be staring down the barrel of one of those infernal guns."

I could feel Julia Moriarty's eyes upon me as she watched intently, waiting for Holmes's reply.

Holmes seemed resolute. "The world cannot turn on possibilities, Watson. A man's life would certainly be forfeit had we not complied."

I seethed inwardly and, in frustration, I looked upwards towards heaven only to see that the cases were now rising above the level of the deck and the crane was preparing to rotate and swing its load towards the gaping maw of the ship's hold.

Just as the crane was beginning to turn, the shrill blast of a ship's whistle from a ferry close by in the Thames gave me a tremendous shock. I thought for a moment my heart had stopped. It seemed to have a galvanising effect on Moriarty's men as weapons had been drawn and they had all fallen onto one knee and into firing positions, ready to repel an assault.

Julia Moriarty had turned and run back to her waiting carriage, apparently ready to flee in the belief that the whistle had been the signal for an ambush. The seconds ticked by and became one and then two tense minutes…but nothing happened. The dockside activities were as before and the crane had continued with its work. It had lowered the cases to their destination and returned to its original position, its engine panting plumes of steam as if tired from its exertions.

Julia Moriarty strode confidently towards us. I noticed that as she did so, she was tucking a nickel-plated revolver back into her handbag. "I should have remembered that you are not a risk taker, Mr Holmes. You will find what you are looking for in Trafalgar Square at four o'clock." With that she turned and boarded her carriage, which was then to be seen leaving at a trot.

Chapter 9 – Mycroft, the whistle blower

I was beside myself. "I cannot believe that Mycroft and the British Government have allowed this. How can they send modern weaponry to a potential enemy with the knowledge that the guns may well be used against British troops? It beggars belief!"

Holmes placed his hand on my shoulder, saying, "It is amazing how restorative a trip on the river can be, Watson," pointing towards a ferry that had just docked.

I looked towards the vessel but I was not to be placated. "That may well be, Holmes, but…Wait! That is Mycroft!"

From the direction of the ferry, a figure approached us that was unmistakably Mycroft Holmes. Not only that but it was plain that he was very pleased with himself for his face was alight with a broad grin.

"It worked perfectly, Sherlock!" and he grasped his brother's arm in an uncharacteristic display of fraternal affection.

I stood speechless; I did not have the faintest notion of what was afoot.

"For pity's sake Holmes, what has happened?" I gasped.

"Watson, old fellow, I have had to deceive you. It was necessary that you were not privy to today's events and that Julia Moriarty believed what she saw. You reacted as I hoped and indeed expected you to do and that gave credibility to our actions."

I was still confused and even more so as I saw the dockside crane lower its hook once more and withdraw from the hold of Mycroft's vessel six wooden crates that were swiftly reloaded onto the wagon.

I could only stand open mouthed and point at the crates as the wagon moved off, back towards the Nordenfelt factory.

Patting me gently on the back, Holmes guided me to our waiting Hansom. "Come Watson, a cup of tea from Mrs Hudson will no doubt be welcome as I explain our little intrigue."

Once back in Baker Street we sat together and Holmes would say nothing until all three of us had a steaming cup of tea in our hands. I could wait no longer; I was bursting to know how the guns could have possibly reappeared.

Holmes sat back and began the explanation. "It is really quite simple, I wanted to fulfil one of Mycroft's boyhood ambitions. He had always wanted to sound the whistle on a steam ship!"

Mycroft laughed and nodded but I was keen to hear what had actually happened.

"I must not tease you so, Watson, for this was a deception that had to work. All had been arranged just as Moriarty had detailed. The guns had to be perfect and functioning, all that we changed was where the dockside crane placed them. Once the guns were raised to deck height, it was necessary to create a little distraction."

Mycroft joined in, saying, "I was aboard the ferry, moored in the centre of the river and alongside the 'Reichstag' but out of sight of the dock. One of my men was in the crane with the driver and once the crates had reached deck height he signalled to me and I sounded the whistle…very enjoyable!"

Holmes continued the explanation. "The distraction was necessary as the crane needed to rotate a little more than it would normally do to load the 'Reichstag'. Whilst Moriarty and her men readied themselves for a suspected assault, the cases were lowered to Mycroft's vessel. Once unloaded, the crane returned empty which satisfied Moriarty."

"Splendid!" I cried, "But what of Edward Martindale and Julia Moriarty?"

Mycroft's tone was now more serious. "Medical attention will be waiting in Trafalgar Square at four o'clock and will escort Edward

Martindale to a private hospital for treatment. As for Julia Moriarty, my men, backed by troops from Woolwich, will storm the house in George Street as soon as they have confirmation that Martindale is safe."

Chapter 10 – George Street

That afternoon was one of the longest that I can remember. We sat and smoked almost continually, jumping up at the slightest noise in the street below. At quarter to five, Holmes began to pace. Suddenly, we heard the ringing of our doorbell. Holmes and I raced downstairs, he snatched the message from a clearly frightened telegram boy whilst I waved him away after pressing a sixpence into his hand. I was still climbing the stairs when I heard Holmes's cry.

"No! It is not possible!" he raved.

I was concerned, saying "What is it Holmes, for pity's sake?"

Holmes was white with rage. "Martindale is safe but Moriarty has escaped!"

I reached down to pick up the telegram that Holmes had thrown to the floor in his anger. It read thus, "Martindale safe and well. Moriarty seen entering house in George Street but not captured when raided, presumed escaped."

"How is this possible Mycroft?" I asked.

Mycroft shook his head, saying, "I don't know, all was in place. My men were to raid the house whilst the Army was to secure the perimeter, letting no one in or out. I must return to Whitehall and procure the detailed reports. I will call upon you again in the morning."

Mycroft nodded to us both and left in haste. I looked towards Holmes, he raged inwardly and could not be consoled. He sat and stayed silent for perhaps an hour before retiring to his room. I sat and tried to read but the shouts and the sounds of furniture being thrown prevented me from concentrating.

Finally, everything became quiet. In my capacity as both friend and physician, I peeped around his door. Holmes was still fully clothed although slumped on the bed. Upon his bedside table were a syringe and a tourniquet. I shook my head in sadness and withdrew to my room. This woman was extorting a terrible price from my friend.

In the morning Mycroft returned after reading the reports of the raid on the house in George Street. Holmes was dressed but was sitting slumped in his old dressing gown, his breakfast tray lying untouched beside him.

Mycroft sat and recounted how the raid had been a success. "From the reports it seems that five armed men had been captured together with a certain Dr Hofmann. On entering the house, my men saw a red-haired woman flee towards the rear. They of course followed but she had disappeared. Once the prisoners had been removed, a thorough search was undertaken but she was nowhere to be found."

I sat back and asked, "How is this possible, Mycroft?"

Mycroft looked a little sheepish. "It would appear that a red-headed woman was stopped by a young trooper in a back alley leading from the house. The woman smiled and raised her skirts to him. The trooper thinking that she was a street girl, told her to be on her way and he let her pass."

A cry of "Idiot!" boomed from across the room. "Could he not have obeyed a simple order? We had her Mycroft! We had her!" Holmes's fist crashed down upon the arm of his chair and he rose, walking towards Mycroft.

Mycroft hung his head. Holmes, on seeing this and recognising that, in truth, it was not his brother's fault, patted him on the arm, saying, "There will be another day and another reckoning, Mycroft. I do not blame you for this." Mycroft slowly looked up and seemed a little cheered by this.

A few moments passed in silent reflection as each of us appeared to turn over the events in our minds. With nothing more to be said, the two brothers shook hands and parted on amicable terms.

It took some time before life returned to some degree of normality. Holmes's anger slowly

162

subsided over the days that followed and about a month later we received a rather cryptic telegram from Mycroft. Mrs Hudson had brought it up on her tray that had proudly sported the new doily destined for our decanter.

Holmes read the telegram before tossing it over to me. "It seems that there are other people interested in the whereabouts of Julia Moriarty."

Opening the telegram I read, "Julia Moriarty is now worth £500 to the Boers after the 'Reichstag' docked without the Maxims."

The author has so far published 10 Sherlock Holmes stories in the short story format so beloved by Sir Arthur Conan Doyle himself. They are available as e-books and may be purchased from all the major on-line bookstores.

The Star of Bithur

The Birchwood Affair

The Cagliari Affair

The Bishop's Tie-Pin

The Rattle-Jacks Affair

The Zhou Bell

The Lymington Affair

The three short stories included in this printed edition are also available as e-book titles.

A collection of his first five books is available as a single e-book entitled

'Sherlock Holmes - The Fireside Collection'

In 2012, his first Science Fiction novel 'Saline' was published as an e-book.

Printed in Great Britain
by Amazon.co.uk, Ltd.,
Marston Gate.